"Nothing's changed, has it? You still want him...still love him."

Jake was about to say something else, but Rosie didn't let him. She was suddenly possessed by an anger, a rage so intense that it overcame her fear of him, her awareness of his contempt and dislike, everything but her need to strike out against him, to make him suffer as she was suffering.

"Love him...? I loathe him...hate him...I've always hated him—always."

PENNY JORDAN was constantly in trouble in school because of her inability to stop daydreaming—especially during French lessons. In her teens, she was an avid romance reader, although it didn't occur to her to try writing one herself until she was older. "My first half-dozen attempts ended up in-gloriously," she remembers, "but I persevered, and one manuscript was finished." She plucked up the courage to send it to a publisher, convinced her book would be rejected. It wasn't, and the rest is history! Penny is married and lives in Cheshire.

Don't miss Penny's latest blockbuster, *Cruel Legacy*, available late 1995.

Books by Penny Jordan

PENNY JORDAN

YESTERDAY'S ECHOES

Harlequin Books

TORONTO • NEW YORK • LONDON
AMSTERDAM • PARIS • SYDNEY • HAMBURG
STOCKHOLM • ATHENS • TOKYO • MILAN
MADRID • WARSAW • BUDAPEST • AUCKLAND

ISBN 0-373-11774-4

YESTERDAY'S ECHOES

First North American Publication 1995.

CHAPTER ONE

'I'M BEGINNING to dread christenings. In fact, I only have to hear the word "baby" these days and I come over all broody...and me a mother of two hulking great teenagers. I ought to know better.

'I know what it is, of course... It's the threat of empty nest syndrome looming, with nothing to look forward to but Greg's mid-life crisis and hormone replacement therapy... Rosie...are you listening to me?'

Obediently Rosie turned towards her elder sister, and repeated obediently what she had just been told.

'Of course, plenty of women are having babies at forty these days,' Rosie heard her muse. 'Although what the kids would have to say about it...and how on earth I'd even manage to get pregnant in the first place... You've no idea how inhibiting it is having almost-adult children in the house with you. It's amazing how guilty and embarrassed they can make you feel. Mind you, talking of sex lives, how's yours going at the moment?'

Rosie felt her stomach muscles tense and prayed that her facial muscles weren't reacting equally betrayingly.

There was virtually a decade between her and her elder sister, and this had led to Chrissie's adopting an almost parental attitude to her. Although Rosie knew that Chrissie would have been outraged had *she* been as inquisitive and critical of her most intimate personal life as Chrissie was of Rosie's, she also knew that Chrissie would never be able to understand that there were times when she found her sister's questions intrusive and over-personal. After all, she knew how much Chrissie loved her and that her questions, no matter how awkward, sprang from love and concern.

And of course today she *was* feeling extra-intensely sensitive, she admitted. Christenings always had that effect on her, and it was pointless expecting Chrissie to understand that, to *know* what she was going through, to *know* about the tearing, wrenching pain within her, the sense of loss and anguish.

It was all very well for Chrissie to talk glibly about feeling broody, about having another child, to assume that she, Rosie, as a single woman of thirty-one with a business to run—a woman who, as Chrissie was always reminding her, had chosen to keep any men who approached her at a wary distance—did not know what it meant to see another woman with a child, and to feel that aching sense of deprivation within her—that tight feeling of panic and pain, of loss and fear, of so many complex emotions that she herself could barely find the words to describe them.

And then for Chrissie to make that comment about her sex life!!

The Hopkinses' lawn wasn't very big; they were a very popular couple and had invited a large number of people to the christening party. Rosie winced as someone standing behind her stepped backwards, and she felt a sharp elbow accidentally striking against her, jolting her glass and causing the other woman to immediately apologise as Rosie automatically turned round.

'I'm so sorry,' she began, but Rosie wasn't listening to her.

Her whole body frozen rigid with shock and rejection, she was staring past her at the man standing several yards away watching her.

Jake Lucas! What was *he* doing here? *Watching* her! She hadn't realised that he knew the Hopkinses. If she had suspected for a moment that *he* was going to be here...

'Rosie...'

She shivered, the rigidity leaving her body as she responded to the quick anxiety in her sister's voice.

Across the space which divided them, Jake Lucas continued to watch her. She could feel the concentrated burn of that look. She knew exactly what he was thinking...how he viewed her...without having to look directly into his eyes.

'Rosie...'

This time Chrissie wasn't content with speaking to her; she was touching her as well—an elder-sisterly hand placed firmly on her arm, giving it an admonishing little shake.

'What is it? What's wrong?'

Wrong? Alarm bells clamoured violently inside her.

'Nothing... Nothing's wrong,' she denied quickly, turning her head back towards her sister so quickly that her hair spun round her, fanning out of its neat, shoulder-length cut before falling silkily back into place, its thick russet sleekness concealing her expression as she lowered her head defensively.

Jake Lucas. Even now that she was no longer looking at him, his features remained burnt into her memory so that it wasn't her sister's firm but anxious face she saw, but his, with its hard, masculine features, his mouth curling disdainfully, his hard, flinty grey eyes watching her with distaste, everything about him, even down to the way he was standing, registering his contempt for her—that and the knowledge of her which they both shared.

'Rosie, what *is* it? And don't tell me nothing. You've gone as white as a sheet,' Chrissie accused. 'Is it the sun? You should have kept your hat on; you know how vulnerable you are to sunstroke. You'd better not drive home.'

Numbly Rosie let her sister's bossy fussing wash over her, for once unable to summon the independence to remind her sister that she was an adult and not one of her children.

'It's time we left, anyway. I promised Greg I wouldn't be late. We've got the Curtises coming round this evening, and I want to make sure that Allison and Paul aren't thinking of going out tonight. I don't like them going out on Sunday evenings, not with Paul's A levels coming up and Allison's GCSEs next year.'

Rosie stayed silent, letting her sister's conversation wash over her. Jake Lucas . . . She tried to remember the last time she had seen him—was it four years ago or three?—but she felt too dizzy with shock to be able to concentrate.

He lived on the opposite side of town from her and their paths never crossed. He moved in different social circles, and the partnership he had in a marina on one of the less accessible Greek islands meant that he was out of the country a good deal.

He was closer to Chrissie's age than her own, although even her redoubtable sister had always been a little in awe of him, despite the fact that she was a couple of years his senior.

He was that kind of man.

Awe didn't describe *her* reaction to him, Rosie acknowledged. Fear . . . dread . . . pain . . . panic . . . anguish; he made her feel all of those, and other and even less bearable emotions as well.

The mere sound of his name was enough to make her go cold with fear and shame, and to see him so unexpectedly, when she was unprepared for it and in such a vulnerable situation, when she was already feeling so off balance, so emotionally open to the anguish of her past and the burden of the pain she had kept a secret from everyone else who knew her...

Silently, she let Chrissie take hold of her arm and firmly make her way through the tightly packed group of people around their host and hostess.

The baby, the Hopkinses' third, was now contentedly asleep in her father's arms. A wrenching jolt of pain stabbed through Rosie as she watched him deftly transfer his new daughter's sleeping weight from one shoulder to the other while he ducked his head to kiss first Chrissie and then her on the cheek.

'Isn't it time we saw you holding one of these?' he teased Rosie.

His teasing wasn't malicious or unkind. Rosie and both Neil and Gemma Hopkins had all been at school together. Gemma was her own age. She herself was, Rosie reminded herself bleakly, the only one of her peers now who had not experienced a committed relationship of some kind. Some of her friends were even on their second marriages.

She knew how curious people were about her, and could guess at the questions they probably asked one another about her. Always sensitive and by nature an extremely private person, she was acutely aware of how different she was, how isolated from experiences which seemed commonplace to others.

It wasn't as though she weren't attractive, as though men weren't drawn to her, Chrissie had exclaimed in exasperation four months ago on Rosie's thirty-first birthday, when she had brought up her perennial complaint about Rosie's dedication to her single state.

'I've watched you,' she had accused. 'You freeze the poor things off as soon as they try to get close to you.'

Her mother had been more understanding, but equally concerned.

'I don't understand it,' she had said sadly. 'Rosie, you were always the one who loved playing with your dolls, who always, from being a small child, talked about getting married and having children. Of the two of you, I always thought it would be Chrissie who would be the career girl. I'm not trying to tell you how to run your life, darling. If being single is what you want...'

'It is,' Rosie had told her mother fiercely, but she suspected that her mother knew as well as she did that she was not telling the whole truth.

But how could she explain, reveal to her mother, to anyone, the thing that had made her like this, the guilt, the pain, the shock of self-discovery, the realisation that her degradation and humiliation, her stupidity, had been witnessed by someone else? These had proved so painful to her that the only way she could deal with them was to try to cut herself off from them, from the person she had been before it had happened, to try to create a different person—a safer, better, more responsible, more controlled person.

How could she tell anyone about what had happened? She was too afraid of them condemning her, looking at her, reacting to her in the same way that Jake Lucas had done.

Over the years she had gone over and over it so many times in her own mind, hating herself for having allowed it to happen, for not being more aware, for not realising what was going to happen.

She knew she was not guilty of ever having done anything to encourage him; she could acquit

herself of that crime. She had never come anywhere near doing or saying anything to make him
think that she might actually want him. How
could she have done? She had not had the least
conception of what sexual desire was.

She had been a very naïve, protected sixteen,
and still far too shy and immature to be sexually
aware in any way.

No, she had done nothing to lead him on, but
she had had that drink and she hadn't been able
to stop him, and she knew enough about the
world now to realise that if she were ever to tell
what had happened there would always be those
who would wonder...doubt...especially if they
were male.

And she could never allow herself to get involved with a man without telling him, without
wanting to share with him that secret, shamed,
still-hurting part of herself.

And since she was afraid of allowing herself
to love a man, only to discover him turning away
from her with the same disgust that Jake Lucas
had manifested, she had chosen instead not to
take the risk of becoming emotionally committed to anyone. It was safer that way, and
safety, protecting herself from hurt—these were
very important to Rosie. When people commented on her manless state, she told them coolly
that she was content the way she was. Normally
the coolness she exhibited, the control, was

enough to deter them and to protect her, but today was different.

Today she was feeling too vulnerable...too raw inside, too achingly aware of that small, sleeping bundle held protectively against Neil's shoulder and the man still standing somewhere among the crowd on the lawn, perhaps still watching her...

She shivered, feeling the perspiration break out against her skin, watching helplessly as Neil's expression changed to one of concern.

'It's the heat,' she heard Chrissie saying. 'She's always been vulnerable to it. It's that red hair and Celtic skin. I told her not to take her hat off.'

There were, Rosie decided faintly as Chrissie led her firmly away, perhaps advantages to having Chrissie for a sister after all.

She quickly changed her mind, though, when Chrissie refused to allow her to drive home.

'But I need my car,' she protested.

'Not now, you don't,' Chrissie told her. 'And if you have got heat or sunstroke, you won't be needing it tomorrow either.'

'I've got a meeting in Chester tomorrow morning,' Rosie protested, but Chrissie wasn't listening.

'Honestly, Rosie, I should have thought at your age you'd know better,' she was complaining as she opened her own car door. 'At times you can be even worse than Paul and Allison... Now get in and I'll take you home. If we didn't have the

Curtises coming round this evening, I'd take you home with me. I know you...'

Sickly, Rosie closed her eyes. She felt as weak and nauseous as if she *were* in fact physically ill, but she knew quite well whatever—or rather, whoever had caused those symptoms.

No matter how much logic she used, her senses, her reactions still continued to remind her of the trauma which lay buried in her past.

Jake Lucas. If only *he* had not been there...that night.

But he had been there...

She winced as Chrissie slammed her car door and started the engine. She was still feeling nauseatingly sick, her body clammy with shock. If only she hadn't already been caught up in the aching pain that seeing the Hopkinses' new baby had caused her, she might have been better able to control her reaction to Jake Lucas, she told herself miserably.

Her sister was still talking, still admonishing her for taking off her hat.

'You left it upstairs on Gemma's bed,' she heard Chrissie reminding her. 'You mustn't forget to collect it when you go back for your car.'

Rosie lived several miles away from her sister and her family. She could well remember the fuss Chrissie had made when she had found out that Rosie was selling her neat, modern flat and buying a run-down, isolated farm worker's cottage.

'It will eat money,' she had warned Rosie. 'And wait until you have to spend a bad winter there. You'll be completely cut off.'

She had frowned disapprovingly at Rosie's *sotto voce* 'Please God' before going on to remonstrate again with her for her foolishness.

'I don't like leaving you here on your own like this,' she said now as she stopped her car in the lane outside the cottage.

'Chrissie, I'll be fine,' Rosie told her wearily. 'Stop fussing. I'm an adult, not a child.'

'You're still my baby sister,' Chrissie told her forthrightly, 'and if you're *that* grown-up, how come you didn't remember to keep your hat on?'

As she got out of the car, Rosie sighed. Typical Chrissie. She always had to have the last word, but beneath her rather bossy manner Rosie knew that Chrissie was genuinely concerned for her and, as she saw that concern now reflected in Chrissie's eyes, her irritation melted away.

'I'll be fine,' she assured her. 'A good night's sleep and——'

'Ring me in the morning,' Chrissie demanded imperatively. 'I'll come over after I've taken Allison and Paul to school and drive you across to collect your car.'

Rosie felt the irritation bubbling up inside her again. She had a meeting in Chester at ten o'clock in the morning. She couldn't afford to hang around waiting for Chrissie to come and collect her, and she certainly wasn't going to cancel. It had taken her months of delicate negotiations to persuade Ian Davies to see her and she wasn't going to throw away everything she had worked so hard for.

She knew that a lot of people had been surprised when she had taken over from her father when he had retired, especially Chrissie. It had been one thing for her to work for him in his insurance agency business, but quite another for her to take over that business and run it single-handedly, despite the fact that she was professionally qualified to do so and had had several years of practical experience, working first for a much larger concern and then, for three years before he retired, for her father.

It had been very hard for her at first, getting the clients to accept her, but then she had managed to deal with a particularly complicated case and get compensation for a client who had come to her after being unable to get satisfaction from his insurance company through another broker. He had been so impressed that he had recommended her to his friends, but breaking down the barriers of male reserve and lack of faith in her abilities was a constant battle.

It didn't help of course that in her normal, everyday life she was so quiet and unassertive, and she had to acknowledge that at barely five feet two, with a very small body frame and a sometimes irritatingly delicate and feminine set of facial features, her physical appearance was perhaps not that of a woman who could withstand the occasionally slightly sneaky tricks adopted by her clients' insurers. Not that they would consider it like that.

Gamesmanship was how they preferred to think of it, a justifiable use of their power, and if someone was weak enough to be browbeaten into giving up a claim or settling for less than they had initially expected then tough luck.

But Rosie had no time for such tactics. She could be surprisingly ruthless and determined when she had to be, but there was no getting away from the fact that in the two years since her father's retirement the business had lost out to some of the much larger agencies.

She had refused to be downhearted; there was still a market ... a need for someone like her who was prepared to give specialised time and attention to a client's needs. The problem was persuading the clients, not convincing herself that her skills were superior to those of a large, faceless organisation.

Which was what she was hoping to do at tomorrow's meeting with Ian Davies.

She had heard in a roundabout fashion that he was dissatisfied with his existing brokers since they had amalgamated with another firm. A fire at one of his rental premises, which had resulted in his full claim being turned down by his insurers, had increased that dissatisfaction, and Rosie had seen her chance and taken it.

He was a contemporary of her father's and, she suspected, not wholly comfortable with women taking a leading role in business. She knew that persuading him to give her his business was not going to be easy, but she was determined to at least try.

To prove to others that she was just as proficient as the equivalent male, or to prove to herself that, just because she was a failure as a woman, it did not mean that she had failed as a human being, that just because she had lost her self-respect, her sense of self-worth, her belief that she was worthy of being loved, it did not mean that every pleasure in life was denied her.

No, not every pleasure, she reflected bitterly. Just the ones she had always taken for granted that she would one day enjoy.

Like being loved and being able to love in return... Like having a child... a family.

As she opened the door and stepped into her small dark hallway, she could feel the angry, impotent tears beginning to sting her eyes.

Damn Jake Lucas... Why had *he* had to be there this afternoon...? Why wouldn't the past let her go? Why couldn't she ever seem to fight free of its destructive tentacles?

CHAPTER TWO

ROSIE waited until she felt comfortably sure that the party would be over and that all the other guests, but most especially Jake Lucas, would have left, and then rang for a taxi. There would be no need for her to disturb the Hopkinses— her car was parked outside their house and not on their drive.

It was just gone nine o'clock when the taxi driver dropped her off, the summer sky still light and the air warm.

Gemma and Neil had been lucky with the weather, Rosie acknowledged as she delved in her handbag for her car keys.

'Aha . . . caught you.'

She tensed automatically and then relaxed as she recognised Neil's teasing voice.

'Gemma saw you arrive,' he told her. 'Why don't you come in for a few minutes?'

Rosie started to protest, but Neil overruled her. A quick search of the road and drive had confirmed that the only other cars there beside her own belonged to Gemma and Neil, and that all the party guests had gone home.

'I didn't want to disturb you,' she started to protest, but Neil had already taken hold of her arm and was coaxing her towards the house.

'There's something we wanted to discuss with you anyway,' he told her. 'Abby has received quite a few gifts of money as christening presents and we were wondering about starting one of these baby bond things for her... What do you think?'

Ten minutes later she was sitting in the Hopkinses' comfortable family kitchen, listening carefully as Gemma outlined their wish to provide some small lump sum for their new daughter when she was older.

The baby herself was fast asleep in Gemma's arms. Neil had gone upstairs to discover what had caused the argument they could hear taking place between their two sons. The phone in the hall rang, causing the baby to stir and cry.

'Here, hold her for me will you please, Rosie, while I go and answer the phone?' Gemma asked her, thrusting the baby towards Rosie so that she had no option other than to take her from her.

She felt warm and solid, with that undefinable but instantly recognisable baby smell.

Tensely Rosie held her, her body rigid, her stomach churning, tremors convulsing her.

Unused to being held at such a distance, and missing the warmth of her mother, the baby's cries increased.

She was still young enough to have that piercing, womb-aching cry of a new baby, and as she heard it Rosie reacted instinctively to it, cradling her against her shoulder, as she supported her small, soft head and soothed her rigid, tense body.

The baby turned her head, nuzzling into Rosie's skin—an automatic reflex action that meant nothing, Rosie knew—and her own body's reaction to it was so immediate and devastating that she could feel herself starting to shake.

Abby had stopped crying now, apparently content with her new surroundings, snuggling sleepily against Rosie's shoulder, but for Rosie to overcome her emotions was not so easy.

She always deliberately avoided this kind of situation, making sure that she had as little physical contact with small babies as she could.

Once they were older it was different, the pain less devastating and primitive, the sense of loss, of deprivation, of agonising guilt, easier to deal with.

She heard Gemma coming back into the kitchen and immediately handed Abby back to her.

'I must go,' she told her quickly. 'I've got an early start in the morning. I'll do some work on some comparison tables for you and drop them around later in the week.'

It was only later, when she was on her way home, that she remembered that in her desperate anxiety to get away she had forgotten all about her hat.

Before going to collect her car she had meticulously gone over and over the proposals she planned to put before Ian Davies.

She was confident that they were at least as competitive as anything anyone could offer him; where she believed *she* had the advantage over much larger concerns was the personal touch.

It was almost eleven o'clock when she went upstairs to prepare for bed. She was just about to get undressed when the phone rang.

It was Chrissie, wanting to know how she was.

Firmly she assured her sister that she was feeling fine but, ten minutes later, when she had removed her make-up and was studying her face in her bathroom mirror, she had to admit that her appearance belied her words.

She had always been pale-skinned, and for that reason had always had to protect her sensitive skin from the sun, but tonight her pallor was sharpened by tension and pain.

Shakily she turned away from the mirror, not wanting to see ... to remember.

Jake Lucas. *He* had remembered. She had seen it in his eyes when he looked at her across the Hopkinses' crowded sun-dappled garden, had seen the coldness and the contempt, the distaste and dislike. It didn't matter *how* hard she worked at burying the past, at shutting herself off from it, at trying to forget it—Jake Lucas would never forget; she could not wipe *his* memory clean, could not erase his knowledge of her.

But at least there was one thing he did not know, one secret that was hers alone.

Rosie winced as she bit down too hard on her bottom lip and broke the skin.

Now she would have a swollen bruise there in the morning. She grimaced crossly in the mirror. She would have to remember to wear a concealing matt lipstick tomorrow. Her mouth was on the over-full side as it was and she had no wish to arrive at Ian Davies's office looking like some pouting little doll.

Before getting in to bed, she checked that she had everything ready for the morning. Her suit was hanging up outside the wardrobe, and so was the silk shirt she intended to wear with it.

Underwear, tights, plus a spare pair in case of accidents, were laid out ready in the bathroom.

Her shoes were downstairs, cleaned and polished, her neat leather handbag-cum-attaché case filled with all the papers she would need.

Rosie did not believe in going for a high-powered female executive image. She felt it both theatrical and off-putting for some of her smaller clients. She preferred to dress neatly and unobtrusively, so that people paid attention to what she had to say, not the way she looked.

She flinched a little, remembering how Chrissie had commented not unkindly, some time ago, that men would never be oblivious to the way she looked.

'They can't help it,' had been her half-indulgent remark. 'It's in their nature, poor dears, and let's face it, Rosie, you are very attractive.'

She had eyed her younger sister judicially before adding, 'In fact, you could be very sexy, if you wanted to be.'

'Well, I don't,' had been Rosie's fierce response.

And it was true. After all, what was the point in looking sexually attractive when she knew how impossible it was for her to follow through the promise of such looks, without at some stage having to reveal the truth.

'Don't think about it,' she warned herself. 'Just accept that that's the way things are. You aren't unhappy. You don't lack for anything.'

Apart from a lover…someone to share her life on an intimate, one-to-one basis. A lover… And a child.

It was the crying that woke her up, bringing her bolt upright in her single, almost monastic little bed, her arms crossing protectively around her body as she tried to clear her brain.

There was the familiar oblong of light cast by the moon through her bedroom window, the familiar pale colours of her simply decorated bedroom with its white bed-linen, its plain, light-coloured walls and carpet, slightly stark against the darkness of the room's oak beams.

She was not, after all, as she had been dreaming, there in that hospital ward, all around her the cries of the new-born babies, to remind her agonisingly of the child she had just lost... The child she had been so terrified she might have conceived, the child she had rejected with panic and shock, terrified of what its conception was going to mean of the way it would alter her life.

But now there was no child, and she was safe. She knew she ought to be glad... relieved. Only somehow she wasn't, and the pain inside her wasn't just caused by the physical shock of the haemorrhage which had preceded her miscarriage. And those piercing new-born cries scraped at her raw nerves like physical torture. No matter what she did, she couldn't escape from him... or from what had happened.

She was shaking, Rosie recognised, her body icy-cold. Even though it was a softly mild night, and despite her shivers her body was drenched in sweat as she fought not to remember.

It was over fifteen years ago now, almost half her own lifetime. She had been sixteen, that was all—still a child in so many ways, and yet still woman enough to grieve tormentedly for the life that was lost, for the child she would never now hold, for the ache within her that came from the emptiness of what she had lost.

Sixteen ... Sixteen, and a virgin. Innocent of any knowledge of male sexuality. And yet she should have known ... should have recognised.

It had been all her own fault, as Jake Lucas had so contemptuously pointed out to her.

You didn't go upstairs with someone, allow him to kiss and fondle you, without knowing where it was going to lead.

Her head had still been thick then with the cider she had had to drink. Only half a glass and she had not finished that, but she learned afterwards that it had been scrumpy, brought back from the south of England by one of the others, with heaven alone knew what added to it.

That still didn't excuse her, though. She shouldn't have drunk it, shouldn't have even been at the party in the first place. If her parents had been at home instead of away at a conference, if her sister had not been staying in the north of England helping her mother-in-law to nurse the husband who was just beginning to recover from a stroke, she would never have been allowed to go.

But they hadn't been there and, out of bravado and a fear of being laughed at by the others, she had given in to her friends' cajoling and agreed to join them.

Tiredly she got out of bed. There was no point in trying to get back to sleep again. Not now.

And no point in reliving the whole thing all over again, she reminded herself bitterly. What good had that ever done, other than to reinforce her feelings of guilt and shame, to conjure up in front of her the sharply vivid mental image of Jake Lucas's cynical, condemnatory expression as he stared down at her half-naked body, the way she lay sprawled across his aunt and uncle's bed?

Then, still in shock, her body still aching with pain, her mind still clouded with alcohol, she had not thought of pregnancy. That had come later in a sickening wave of panic and rejection, when she'd realised that she could have conceived.

She hadn't told anyone; she had been too afraid, too aware by then of her own guilt and degradation.

A month went by and the panic became a certainty, but still she did nothing.

All around her life went on as normal, and she felt somehow that if she pretended it had simply not happened . . . if she said and did nothing, it would all magically go away. That the nausea she felt in the morning would stop, that her body's rhythms would return to normal, that the mental pictures that filled her brain at night while she slept would disappear, and that she would once again be the girl she had been before.

No one said anything to her; no one seemed to be aware of what had happened.

Jake Lucas's aunt and uncle had emigrated to Australia three weeks after the party, with their family.

Some days she almost managed to convince herself that it had never happened, and then something would remind her: she would see a woman pushing a pram on her way home from school...or see a small baby on television. Whenever she saw a heavily pregnant woman she found herself looking the other way, as the panic bubbled up inside her.

Her mother was concerned about her and feared that she had been studying too hard for her exams.

The guilt she felt when she heard this was the worst kind of punishment. Her parents loved and trusted her. How could she tell them the truth?

And then, while they were away visiting friends and Chrissie was still with her mother-in-law, it happened.

Rosie had gone in to Chester for the day. She had some books she wanted to buy which were not available in their small market town.

She had bought the books and had just been walking out of the shop when it happened—a pain so searing and sharp that she dropped the books, her hand instinctively going to her stomach as she collapsed.

When she came round it was all over and she was in hospital.

She had lost her baby, a harassed young doctor had told her briskly, and they wanted to keep her in overnight just to check that there were no complications.

After that everyone seemed to ignore her, and it was only later that she learned that there had been an emergency that evening, with a major road accident locally.

In the confusion of that, no one realised that Rosie's family had not been advised of what had happened, and when Rosie was discharged from the hospital the next day with a clean bill of health she realised numbly that no one but her knew or needed to know what had happened.

At first she was overwhelmed with relief and gratitude for that fact, but later, when the sound of crying babies brought her out of her sleep, when the guilt over what she had done was replaced by the far greater guilt and anguish of having lost her child, she ached for someone to talk to, someone to confide in, someone with whom she could share her confused feelings.

Logically she knew that her miscarriage was probably the best thing that could have happened. She was sixteen years old, she had attended a party without her parents' knowledge, had had too much to drink and as a result . . . She shuddered, still not able to contemplate what had actually happened, and yet, despite knowing all that, she had still grieved for her lost child.

And still did.

She went downstairs and filled the kettle so that she could make herself a drink of herbal tea. Perhaps that might help her to get back to sleep.

She knew now that she would never have another child. How could she risk another man looking at her the way Jake Lucas had looked at her, when she told him about her past? She was too proud to want a relationship in which it remained a secret—that was not her ideal of marriage, of commitment, of sharing.

Once she realised what was happening she had, of course, tried to stop him, but he had pinned her to the bed, leaving dark bruises on her arms as he forced his way into her body, making her cry out in shock, not just at his unwanted, forced physical possession of her, but also at the emotional humiliation and degradation she was being made to suffer.

It had all been over within seconds, but those seconds had been long enough to change her life irretrievably. Even now, remembering ... thinking about what had happened, Rosie was filled with self-disgust and guilt.

She had withdrawn into herself afterwards, earning for herself a reputation as a swot, as someone who would rather stay at home with her family than go out with her friends.

Her sense of shame and guilt over what had happened was so strong that she could not bear anyone else to know what she had done.

Rather then endure a repeat of the humiliation and shame, the sense of anguished guilt she had already known, she decided that her life must have another focus, that for the sake of her own sanity and self-respect she must accept that that commitment—marriage, a relationship that included a lover and the children they might have together—was not for her.

And most of the time she managed to convince herself that she was content. Except when she saw a small baby or a pregnant woman, except when she woke in the night remembering the past, except when something or someone reminded her of what had happened.

Her tea had gone cold. She looked at it with distaste.

It was fortunate that she was not superstitious, she told herself bitterly, because there could be no worse omen to precede her meeting with Ian Davies than what had happened today.

Tiredly she went back to bed, promising herself that this time she was not going to allow Jake Lucas to disturb her much-needed rest. That this time she was not going to lie there in the darkness remembering the way he had looked at her, the way he had spoken to her, the contempt and dislike with which he had treated her.

This would have to happen to her today of all days, Rosie fumed anxiously, as she waited on the full garage forecourt for a petrol pump to become free.

After all the careful preparations she had made for this morning's meeting with Ian Davies, how on earth had she come to overlook something as vital as making sure her petrol tank was full?

The pump in front of her became free and she pulled quickly into it, ignoring the attempts of the driver behind her to cut in ahead of her.

As she unlocked the petrol cap and pushed the nozzle of the hose into the tank, for some contrary reason, instead of gushing smoothly into the tank, the strong-smelling liquid flooded backwards, spilling out on to her shoes and tights...

It was only a few small splashes, but they left a dismaying strong smell, Rosie acknowledged as she queued to pay for her petrol.

She always left herself with a good extra margin of time when she was travelling to an appointment, but this morning everything seemed to be against her. She had lost at least fifteen minutes getting petrol, and once she was actually on the motorway there was an unexpected hold-up where a lorry had shed its load and the mess was being cleaned up. She eventually arrived in Chester with only five minutes in which to find a parking spot and to get to Ian Davies's offices, and Chester was a notoriously difficult place to park.

Luckily she found a spot just when she was beginning to panic and fear that she was going to be late, and even more luckily she found in the glove compartment a long-forgotten bottle of body lotion which a friend had given her to pass on to Chrissie for one of her jumble collections.

As she used it to clean the petrol stains and smell off her legs and shoes, Rosie winced a little at its strong scent. It was a perfume designed to be worn in the evening, not during the day, and it was certainly far too strong for her taste, but at least it had removed the malodorous smell of petrol.

She reached the offices with a minute to spare, and self-consciously checked her appearance in the lift mirror, to see if she looked as flushed and untidy as her hurried rush through the centre of Chester had made her feel.

A little to her own surprise, the reflection that stared back at her from the small mirror looked cool and composed.

Idly, as she waited for the lift to carry her to the top floor, she wondered if anyone had ever thought of placing a hidden camera or watching device in a lift, and then, remembering some of the very odd things she had heard that people sometimes got up to inside them, she reflected wryly that it was probably just as well they did not.

The lift doors opened and she stepped out into the carpeted foyer, composing her features into a calm, professional smile.

The meeting proved every bit as tricky as she had expected. Ian Davies was a chauvinist who, Rosie suspected, did not entirely approve of the new role that women were playing in the business world.

Had she been a secretary, a personal assistant, someone's wife or woman friend, she had no doubt that he would have been perfectly charming to her and perhaps even have flirted with her in a courtly, old-fashioned sort of way, but it was plain to her that he was antagonistic not so much to her, but to what she represented.

But, for all his prejudices, he was still very much a business man, and Rosie saw how quickly ne assimilated the advantages of using her as his broker.

'Are you saying that, had you had our business, you would have got us more compensation from our insurers?' he asked her at one point.

Firmly Rosie shook her head. She was not going to be caught out like that.

'Without knowing the full details of the arrangements your previous brokers had with your insurers, I can't say that,' she told him equably, but smiling, a little grimly, inwardly to herself as she saw that he had caught the small hint she had dropped about his brokers' private arrangements with the insurers.

She had a very shrewd idea that the brokers he was presently using adopted a policy which she herself refused to consider, and that was an agreement to let some claims go through unhindered in return for the brokers advising other clients not to proceed with theirs, or suggesting to them they should accept lower compensations.

It was her view that her primary loyalty was to her clients and, if that meant a less easy passage with some of the insurance companies, well, so be it.

'I've brought some comparison quotes with me,' she told him as she stood up. 'If I may, I'll leave them with you.'

A little to her surprise, he accompanied her out into the foyer, but after she had thanked him crisply for his time and turned round to leave she realised why.

Jake Lucas was seated in the foyer, obviously waiting to see him, because he was now standing up, and beyond her she could hear Ian Davies saying something about taking him to lunch.

For a moment the shock of seeing him had paralysed her completely, and then Rosie turned quickly on her heel, her heart hammering furiously fast as it drove the blood through her veins, overheating her pale skin.

She felt hot and sick, filled with panic and a frantic desire to escape. It had been bad enough seeing him yesterday, but this was worse.

Frantically she tried to cling to her self-control and professionalism, but in her haste to escape she moved too quickly, and the papers she was carrying slid from her hot, tense grasp.

She bent immediately to pick them up, her face flushing with angry mortification, and then, to her horror, she realised that two pages of paper had drifted to where Jake Lucas was standing.

For a moment she was too panic-stricken to move, and could only crouch where she was, staring numbly at them, filled with sickness and terror at the thought of having to retrieve them.

When Jake himself bent down and picked them up she could only stare at him, unable to drag her gaze from the flat metallic hardness of his grey eyes—like a rabbit trapped by a car's headlights, she thought mechanically, as he came towards her.

She struggled to stand up, and then completed her self-humiliation by half losing her balance.

The shock of Jake's hand curling round her arm was like a jolt of electricity. He was so close to her that she could see the dark line along his jaw where he shaved, smell the crisp, clean scent of his soap, see the masculine curl of the dark hairs on his arm where his wrist protruded from his shirt sleeve.

He was still holding her, still watching her... Do something, her brain screamed frantically. *Do something* ...

Somehow she managed to find the will-power to get to her feet, but, as she did so, either because of her tension or the heat it had generated, she was suddenly sharply conscious of the smell of the body lotion she had used to clean her legs, and, she realised, Jake Lucas was aware of it too... She saw the slight, and very betraying, fastidious twitch of his nose, the way his eyes narrowed, the brief, downward glance he gave the lower half of her body and, while she automatically thanked him for his help and turned quickly to make her escape, she was sickly aware of the contempt that faint curl of his mouth had carried.

The look he had given her as she dragged her arm away from his grip had underlined that contempt.

He had never made any attempt to hide from her what he thought of her: that he thought she was sexually promiscuous, that she used her body as a means of getting what she wanted out of life... out of men. And he had just let her know quite plainly that by scenting her legs with that strong, voluptuous perfume she was amply confirming his judgment of her.

What business woman who wanted to be taken seriously at a professional level did anything like that? A discreet touch of something light and cool, a subtle message that said that she was a woman and proud of that fact—that was permissible and acceptable. To wear something so heavy and voluptuous gave off a very different message indeed.

On her way down in the lift, Rosie studied her reflection again. This time it was very different. Her face was flushed, especially along her cheekbones, her eyes huge and dark with emotion, the pupils enormously dilated. Even her mouth looked different somehow, softer, fuller... as though... as though she had been kissed.

Shuddering with distaste, she turned away, and when she stepped out into the street she acknowledged that she felt so emotionally raw and on edge that she was on the verge of tears.

It was just disappointment because Ian Davies had not responded more enthusiastically to her approach, she told herself as she walked back to her car. It wasn't anything to do with seeing Jake Lucas. That *had* upset her of course, but she wasn't going to let the fact that he despised her, that he was contemptuous of her, reduce her to tears.

It wasn't, after all, his judgment of her that hurt so much; it was the fact that seeing him always reminded him so unbearably of what she had done, of the way *she* had demeaned herself.

It was bad enough that *she* knew of her shame and degradation, without him having to know of it too.

But he did know, and nothing she could do could ever erase that knowledge. When he looked at her, she knew as surely as though he were saying the actual words that he was seeing her not as she was now, but as she had been then, half-naked, stupid with drink and shock, lying across his aunt and uncle's bed, while her partner, the boy who had deliberately given her that spiked drink and who had then equally deliberately semi-coaxed and semi-dragged her upstairs to his parents' bedroom, had left her, after telling her triumphantly that he had won his bet to seduce her and bring her down off her high horse.

He had not said that to his cousin, though. No, it was a very different story he had told Jake

Lucas. According to him, she had been willing, and more than willing, to accompany him upstairs—she had been the one to suggest it, in fact, and Rosie, too shocked and distressed to defend herself, too humiliated physically and emotionally, had done nothing to defend herself.

Thank God that Ritchie Lucas and his family had emigrated to Australia so quickly afterwards.

And thank God also that Ritchie had apparently got so drunk that evening that it had appeared that he had no recollection of what had taken place and so had been unable to boast to anyone else about it.

No, only two people had remembered what had happened—herself and Jake Lucas—and Jake Lucas did not know the real truth.

He had assumed that she was a member of the rather wild crowd that Ritchie went around with, that she was one of those girls who was foolishly experimenting with sex and drink in the mistaken belief that she was showing everyone how grown-up she was and, beneath his anger at his cousin for taking advantage of his parents' absence to throw an unauthorised party, and his obvious disgust that Ritchie had brought her upstairs to his parents' room, Rosie had been sharply conscious of the contempt he had for her.

And yet his judgement of her couldn't have been further off the mark. She had never even kissed a boy properly before that night, never mind done anything else, and, if it hadn't been that for the previous few months a small group of girls in her class at school had been making her life a misery by taunting her about her 'primness' and her 'goody-goodyness' to the extent that she was slowly becoming alienated from all the other girls and treated as someone who was 'different'... an outcast, she doubted that she would ever have allowed herself to be persuaded to even go to the party in the first place.

To discover later that she had been the subject of a cruel trick deliberately planned to hurt and humiliate her had been hard to bear, but not as hard as Jake Lucas's contempt, and certainly not as hard as discovering that she was pregnant.

At least no one but her knew about that. She bit her lip as she bent to unlock her car door, hot tears stinging her eyes.

There had been no one to grieve with her over the loss of that baby, no one to share her complex and conflicting emotions, no one to tell that, while logically she knew that perhaps it was all for the best, a part of her ached with loss and pain for that unborn child.

No, that was something that no one else knew, and sometimes she wished they did... sometimes she ached inside to be able to talk about what she had experienced: her pain, her sense of loss... her sense of guilt.

Despite the fact that it was over fifteen years ago since it had happened, sometimes she felt as close to it as though it were less than fifteen weeks, as though the wound, the agony, was still so raw that she needed to be able to talk it through with someone . . . that she needed to be able to publicly and openly mourn the death of her child.

But someone like Jake Lucas would never be able to understand those kind of emotions. She could just imagine his reaction. No doubt he would have told her that she was lucky things had worked out as they had, that such luck was far in excess of what she actually deserved. He would have no pity, no compassion . . . no understanding... He would reject her pain and her need to express it in just the same contemptuous way as he had rejected her, turning away from her to talk to his cousin, ignoring her as though she simply did not exist.

But he had come to see her afterwards.

Yes, she told herself savagely, to make sure she wasn't going to make any trouble for his precious cousin.

Angrily she put the car in gear and reversed out of her parking spot.

CHAPTER THREE

'ANY luck with Ian Davies?'

Rosie looked wryly at her brother-in-law.

'Well, I haven't heard anything from him yet, but he didn't give me the impression that he was interested. He's one of those men who isn't really comfortable with women holding positions of authority in business. If Dad had still been running things, it might have been different.' She gave a small shrug. 'Still, it's his loss as much as ours. I suspect his existing brokers are using his business to get better terms for their other clients instead of reducing his premiums.'

'Did you tell *him* that?' Chrissie demanded.

Rosie shook her head.

'I only suspect that that's what they're doing,' she told her.

'Well, I think it's all wrong that men should still try to keep women down,' Allison announced passionately with indignation. At fourteen she was just beginning to lay claim to her independence, and was staunchly pro women's rights.

'I wonder how Gran and Grandad are getting on. They'll be in Japan now, won't they?' Paul chimed in.

'Yes, they should have arrived there by now,' Rosie agreed.

'I never thought they'd actually do it,' Chrissie marvelled. 'Spending a whole year travelling round the world.'

'It's something they've been planning for and dreaming about for years,' Rosie reminded her.

Chrissie had rung her earlier in the day to check that she was going round as usual to have supper with them, a regular Friday night ritual which Rosie always enjoyed.

'Did you collect your hat from the Hopkinses?' Chrissie asked her now.

'No, not yet,' Rosie told her.

'There's a car boot sale on tomorrow morning. Fancy coming?'

Rosie shook her head.

'I can't. I've promised to go over and see Mary Fuller to help her fill out some claim forms. Her garage was broken into on Wednesday and some things stolen.'

She stood up to leave and was surprised when Chrissie reached out to detain her.

'Not yet,' she muttered. 'There's something I want to tell you. Allison, Paul, upstairs both of you, to make a start on your homework,' she instructed her children.

Rosie frowned as her brother-in-law, too, disappeared from the kitchen, saying something about having a phone-call to make.

Chrissie had been on edge all evening, flustered and quick-tempered in a way which was out of character for her, and immediately they were on their own Rosie demanded anxiously, 'What is it? What's wrong?'

When Chrissie sat down, her eyes filling with tears, Rosie stared at her.

'Chrissie,' she exclaimed reaching out towards her. 'What is it?'

'I'm pregnant,' Chrissie told her tearfully. 'I've only found out this morning. I thought it was just my age… I mean, I *am* forty…but I've been feeling so uncomfortable, so bloated and sick, that I decided I'd go and see Dr Farrar. When she asked me if I could possibly be pregnant, I laughed at first…

'Oh, Rosie, what on earth are people going to say? Allison and Paul? I feel such a fool. A baby at my age… Would you believe it? Greg is thrilled… Isn't that just like a man?' she complained as she sniffed and blew her nose vigorously.

'I'm sorry about that,' she apologised. 'It's just been such a shock…'

'You're not that old,' Rosie assured her automatically. 'Lots of women have babies at your age, some of them for the first time, and as for

Allison and Paul... You wait... I'm sure they'll understand.'

Chrissie pregnant... Chrissie having a baby... Although outwardly she knew she appeared calm, her words warm and soothing, inwardly her reaction was very, very different.

She could not be *jealous* of Chrissie, she told herself later as she drove home, having congratulated her slightly shamefaced brother-in-law who, as Chrissie had said, was quite obviously thrilled at the idea of another child.

Jealous of Chrissie... She could not be... She *must* not be. And yet, as she parked her car outside her own home, she acknowledged that she was.

Not jealous in the way that one might be of someone else's material possessions or even someone else's apparently more fortunate lifestyle; no, this jealousy wasn't like that—it went deeper, bit more sharply, hurt her in so many different ways that she almost felt as though she wanted to scream her pain and misery to the world.

It wasn't that she didn't want Chrissie to have her baby. She shuddered at the thought. It was just... It was just that she... It was just that she what? Wanted a child of her own. A child she would have to bring up single-handedly. A child to whom she would one day have to explain and apologise for its lack of a father. Was that what she really wanted?

She didn't know what she wanted, she acknowledged later; all she did know was that the control she had always been so careful to exercise over herself and her deepest innermost feelings was dangerously close to splintering. That the pain she had thought she had buried so deep that it would never, ever surface was growing inside her, threatening to overwhelm her.

She must not let it. She must not let anyone... anyone guess what she was feeling, especially Chrissie who, for all her strength, was right now feeling very vulnerable, and who needed her love and support.

In the morning she woke up heavy-eyed and on edge. Her sleep had been disturbed by confusing, unhappy dreams from which she had woken up with tears on her face.

She must stop this, she told herself as she prepared to go and see her client. She had heard about, read about women who became obsessed with their need to fulfil their primary biological function and have a child. It filled and sometimes destroyed their whole lives, occupying them to such an extent there was no room left for other things, other relationships which might have offered them comfort and compensation.

But, deep down inside her, Rosie knew that it wasn't so much the desire to have a child that was causing her emotional anguish, but that somehow her feelings were all connected with the child she could have had but had lost. It was not just that she felt pain and on her own behalf; she felt it on that child's as well. Pain and guilt, sorrow, anger almost, because her child had never been properly grieved for, had never been allowed to be acknowledged... because she had never been able to mourn its loss and share what she was feeling with others.

But how could she have shared it? To share it would have meant admitting what had happened, revealing what she had done, how she had behaved.

Did she really want other people to know about that? Look how Jake Lucas had reacted. Did she really want to see that same contempt in other people's eyes, to know that people were talking about her behind her back, discussing what she had done...? And besides, it was all too late, over fifteen years too late.

But no matter how logically she tried to argue with herself, she still felt emotional and on edge. The thought of having to spend the next eight months or so listening to her sister talking about her pregnancy and making plans for the eventual birth of her baby made her stomach churn with tension and anxiety.

She felt as though emotionally she was stretched so tightly, so over-wound inside, that she was almost on the verge of snapping completely.

What had happened to her? This time last week she had been perfectly all right... Hadn't she? All right, so she hadn't wanted to attend the Hopkinses' christening, and thinking about it had brought everything back, resurrected the pain she was increasingly conscious of having to suppress, but she had been to other christenings and had coped. What had been so special about this one, other than the fact that Jake Lucas had been there?

Jake Lucas. It was *his* fault she was feeling like this, she decided bitterly. It was because of him that she couldn't enjoy the news of her sister's pregnancy, couldn't react with the unshadowed pleasure and enthusiasm she wanted to feel.

Jake Lucas... If only he hadn't been there that night... If only he hadn't opened the door and seen... It had all been over then anyway, her frightened struggles to escape from his cousin's too powerful grip long since subdued and the damage done.

Jake Lucas. She hated and loathed him almost as much as he despised her. She smiled bitterly to herself. Much he would care. Still, she very much doubted that he was used to being on the receiving end of such a negative emotion from her sex. He was, physically at least, a very attractive and compelling man—even she could see that—the kind of man she would have expected to have had a string of women passing through his life, but oddly he seemed not to do so. He had a wide social circle of friends, but if he had a serious personal relationship with anyone it had not reached the town's very efficient grapevine.

Good-looking, comparatively wealthy and, according to everyone else, with the kind of personality that immediately drew others towards him, he still remained single.

'Rumour has it that he fell in love with someone years ago and that he's never got over it,' Chrissie had once remarked, but Rosie had found it hard to believe her. Jake Lucas, in love? He was too hard, too detached, his opinion of himself far too high to allow him to admit into his life the turbulence of an emotion like love.

It took most of the morning for her to help her client fill in her claims forms. The burglary had upset her, and left her feeling nervous and insecure, and Rosie, who had come across the same thing with other clients who had suffered similar robberies, let her talk, knowing that this was the best thing she could do.

Would she have felt any different, would her life been any different, if there had been someone for her to talk to? But how did you tell someone, anyone, anything like that? To explain what had happened, how her baby had been conceived in the first place, would have been hard enough, but then to go on to discuss her mixed and contradictory feelings over her miscarriage... How could she tell *anyone* of the relief she had first felt... relief at the death of her child, and then go on to expect them to believe how later her feelings had changed completely, and how guilty she had felt? As though in some way she had actually willed the miscarriage on herself.

Had there been any repercussions? Jake Lucas had asked her curtly the day he had come to see her.

'No,' she had told him stoically, denying the truth, keeping it secret and hidden, just as she had gone on keeping it secret and hidden ever since; but she had lied: there had been repercussions then and there still were now, echoing agonisingly through her life, through her.

These days there was counselling available to people who suffered trauma, but at sixteen she had been too young, and much too ashamed and frightened, to have sought out any kind of professional advice even if she had been aware that she could have done so.

All she had wanted to do when she left the hospital was to put the whole thing behind her, to lock it away in the darkest, most hidden recesses of her mind, where it could lie forgotten.

Only her guilt had not allowed her to forget it; it had driven her, relentlessly sharpened by pain. And it had been a twofold guilt.

Initially she had felt shame and anxiety because of what she had done because, even though she knew they would do all they could to help her, her parents would be hurt. She had not thought about the baby then, that had come later...a secondary and much, much worse guilt, a deep, more intense feeling of having failed another human being, of having let them down and caused them to suffer. Her baby had died and, even though logically she knew such things happened, she still felt that she was to blame, that somehow her baby had known that it was not loved...not wanted and that because of that...

And now Chrissie was having a third child. Rosie gripped the steering-wheel tightly.

She was not going to allow herself to be envious of her sister, to spoil the relationship she had with her with feelings of useless envy, to spoil the relationship she would one day have with her new niece or nephew with unhappiness for the child she had lost.

It was just gone lunchtime when she got home. On Saturday morning she normally got up early and drove into town to do her food shopping, while everywhere was relatively quiet, but today, because of her business appointment, that had not been possible, and now she realised she was virtually out of fresh food.

Not that it mattered. She didn't really feel very hungry.

But she really ought to have something to eat, an inner voice nagged her. Neglecting her health wasn't going to solve anything or make her feel any better, was it?

Grimly she pulled open the fridge door and surveyed its contents without any real enthusiasm and then closed it again.

The hot, sunny weather had continued all week, and her garden, especially the pots of flowers and herbs by the back door, all needed watering.

Originally built to house farm workers, her cottage had a very good-sized rear garden, which had been one of the main reasons Rosie had bought it in the first place.

Last summer, much to Chrissie's exasperation, she had painstakingly laid a pretty, small, stone-paved area outside the back door.

It had taken up virtually all her spare time for the whole of the summer, and Chrissie had told her forthrightly that she would have been wiser to pay someone else to do the work, leaving herself with enough free time to concentrate on her own social life.

'Honestly, Rosie,' she had told her. 'Anyone would think you *wanted* to be on your own.

Every time anyone asks you for a date you tell them that you can't because you're working on that patio.'

Rosie had said nothing, not wanting to admit to her sister that inadvertently she had hit upon the truth.

Rosie assumed that it was because her job brought her into contact with so many men that she was constantly being asked out, unaware that it was her looks and personality that were really responsible for their interest.

'What's wrong with you?' Chrissie had demanded with sisterly candour.

'I just don't want to get involved,' Rosie had responded quietly.

Outwardly she had been calm, and even slightly withdrawn, but only because that was the sole way she had of controlling her inner pain.

She ached to be able to confide in her sister, to tell her what she was suffering, but she had been too embarrassed, and besides, keeping her emotions, her fears, the truth hidden had become so much a part of her that the mere thought of discussing it with anyone else caused her to feel acute terror and panic.

Instead of having some lunch she made herself a cup of coffee and then, changing into her jeans and a T-shirt, she went outside and connected up the hose-pipe.

She had a small vegetable plot which she was diligently tending at the bottom of the garden.

She was working busily in it and just starting to relax, enjoying the warmth of the sun and the peace, when suddenly she heard children's voices as some people walked past, and immediately she began to feel her tension return.

This was getting ridiculous, she told herself shakily, as she put down her fork. *She* was getting ridiculous.

Even so, she couldn't stay where she was. She hurried back to the house, angry with herself and frightened at the same time. If she couldn't bear to hear the sound of other people's children, things were getting worse, she acknowledged as she stripped off her gardening gloves outside the back door. It was the news about Chrissie's baby that had thrown her into this mood, but somehow she must come to terms with it to...

She tensed as she heard someone walking down the path that ran alongside her house.

She heard the gate squeak as it was opened, and firm, male footsteps.

She moved forward to see who her visitor was at the same moment as he came round the corner.

Jake Lucas!

Rosie froze.

'I couldn't get any answer when I rang the bell at the front,' she heard him saying. 'But your car was outside, so I thought I'd just check to see if you were in the garden.'

The shock was beginning to recede now, slowly and painfully, so that it was as though her numbed brain was only gradually coming back to life; her thought processes were slow and disjointed.

'I've brought you this. You left it at the Hopkinses' last weekend.'

Rosie stared at the hat he was holding in his hand. Her hat.

She lifted her head and looked at his face.

Why had Jake Lucas brought her hat back? What was he doing here? What did he want?

Suddenly her thoughts began to accelerate and then to skid frantically out of control as panic gripped her.

'There's something else I wanted to discuss with you as well.'

His voice was deep and calm...controlled... but Rosie still caught the note of hidden tension within it, her perceptions sharpened by her own tension and fear.

'There isn't anything you and I could possibly have to discuss,' she told him fiercely.

It was too much, his coming round here like this, invading her privacy, her peace...just as his memory constantly invaded her thoughts... her dreams...or, rather, her nightmares.

She saw that he was frowning and her heart gave a frantic bound, but she wasn't going to let him intimidate her any more with his disdain...his contempt...

Like her he was dressed casually in jeans and a cotton T-shirt but, where hers was large and loose, his clung lovingly to a torso that was surely far too athletically, firmly muscled for a man of close to forty.

His arms—tanned, no doubt by the time he spent in Greece—made his T-shirt look even whiter in contrast.

It was all very well knowing that pale skin was far healthier, safer than that which was tanned, but even so she couldn't help contrasting the cream pallor of her own arms with the warm golden-brown of his, and feeling slightly envious, Rosie admitted.

As she spoke, she stretched out her hand to take her hat from him, making no attempt to conceal her hostility and bitterness.

Why should she, after all? *He* had never made any attempt to conceal how he felt about her. She made it plain by her body language that she expected him to hand over her hat and leave without saying whatever it was he seemed to think they had to discuss. But, instead of responding to the message of her tense muscles and shuttered face, he kept hold of her hat and took a step further into the garden, a step closer to her, so that her fingertips accidentally brushed against the flesh of his forearm.

His skin felt warm and smooth like velvet, so that for a moment she was actually tempted to stroke it and savour the pleasure it gave her to touch it. The dark hair covering his skin was much softer than she had expected. Somehow she had thought it must feel abrasive... Because that was how she saw him? Instead it felt silkily fine, distracting and confusing her.

The sensation of him jerking his arm away from her touch, just a heartbeat before she herself removed her fingers, made her face burn with shamed confusion and panic.

She should have been the one to withdraw first, instead of standing there, practically caressing him deliberately. As though... as though... as though she had actually wanted to touch him. And that would be what he was thinking of course... That she hadn't changed at all... that she was still the person he had believed her to be at sixteen, and so avaricious for sensual, sexual sensation that she would offer herself to any male... initiating intimacy where none was wanted.

'Ritchie is coming back.'

She was so wrapped up in her own anger that it was several seconds before she realised what he had said, what the hard, flatly delivered short sentence actually meant.

When she did she reacted automatically, shock turning her skin even paler, as she stepped back from him instinctively, looking directly into his face, searching it frantically, half expecting to find he was simply tormenting her. But, as she met his eyes, she saw that he was speaking the truth.

Her heart started beating frantically fast, her stomach churning nauseously.

'Why... How?'

She seemed to hear her own voice from outside her body, thin and weak, taut with tension, as fear and shock poured reactively through her.

She could see the way Jake's mouth curled fastidiously with disdain, the way he stepped back from her, almost as though he believed she actually contaminated the air between them, as though he couldn't bear to be anywhere near her.

'He's married,' he told her harshly. 'He's coming over on business and decided to combine it with a holiday. He's bringing his wife and children with him. His wife wanted to see the place where he grew up.'

Children... Ritchie Lucas had children... Just for a moment she was so overwhelmed by bitterness and pain that she almost cried out, and then thankfully the agony faded, and with it the red mist of fury which had momentarily possessed her.

'Nothing's changed, has it?' she heard Jake saying in angry disgust. 'You still want him...still love him.'

He was about to say something else, but Rosie didn't let him.

She was suddenly possessed by an anger, a rage so intense that it overcame her fear of him, her awareness of his contempt and dislike, everything but her need to strike out against him, to make him suffer as she was suffering...to refute...

It boiled and raged inside her, demanding an outlet, refusing to be suppressed any longer. She was literally shaking with the force of it when she opened her mouth and told him wildly. 'Love him...? I loathe him...hate him... I've always hated him—always.'

She was shaking violently now, barely aware of the small, frantic voice inside urging her to be more cautious, but suddenly she needed to vent her emotions, her bitterness, to tell Jake Lucas how she felt, how she hurt.

It was as though the injustice of his accusation, coming on top of all that she was already suffering, had driven everything but her need to defend herself from it out of her mind.

'How *could* I love him after what he did to me? The way he forced himself on me...the way he ruined my life...?'

She was crying now, raising her hand to dash the tears away impatiently as the rage continued to burn through her, fuelling the hot outburst of everything she had kept locked inside herself for so long.

'Ritchie *forced* himself on you...?'

The sharp question sliced through her hysteria, shocking her into silence.

She was shivering, ice-cold with shock and reaction, Rosie realised shakily, as the icy disbelief in Jake Lucas's voice cut through the heat of her emotional outburst.

'Are you trying to claim that Ritchie raped you?' he demanded acidly. 'Because if so...'

Nausea clawed at her stomach. She had to stretch out an arm towards the wall of the house to support herself and yet, despite the terror, the fear rising up inside her, despite the vivid image etched on her brain of the way this man had stood and watched her as she lay rigid on his aunt and uncle's bed, her still only youthfully developed breasts partly revealed to him, her body numb with panic and shock but her brain, her emotions rawly vulnerable to the contempt, the disgust with which he was regarding her, Rosie suddenly knew that if she backed down now, if she allowed him to use her vulnerability and pain against her so that he could reject the truth, she would suffer for that weakness for the rest of her life. She had made that mistake once; she wasn't going to make it a second time.

Curling her fingers into the window sill, she willed herself to be strong, to stand up for herself. She was a woman now, not a child.

'Because if so what?' she challenged him bitterly. 'You'd be more than happy to stand up in court and call me a liar...' Her mouth trembled, but grimly she fought for control. 'Maybe Ritchie didn't knock me unconscious and drag me up-stairs...and of course, to a man like you, that is what rape constitutes, isn't it...'

'You were drunk,' Jake interrupted her flatly. He had gone pale beneath his tan, she noticed, and his eyes, the eyes she had always thought of as being so cold and unemotional, were blazing with heat.

Somehow this sign that he was, after all, capable of betraying himself with human emotion instead of making her afraid that he might lose his temper actually strengthened her determination to stand up for herself.

'Yes,' she agreed. 'Because my drink had been spiked... Deliberately, as I discovered later.' Her mouth twisted a little. 'By my so-called friends with the connivance of your cousin.' Her head lifted proudly as she tilted it back so that she could look directly at him. 'Apparently your cousin thought that it was high time I learned what life...what sex was all about...' Distaste shadowed her eyes as she looked away from him. 'So, yes, I was drunk... Mercifully... But not so much that I didn't know what was happening——'

'Just enough to ensure that you didn't do anything to stop it, is that what you're saying?'

The harshness of his voice made Rosie's skin burn.

'If Ritchie did, as you claim, force you... then why the hell didn't you say something at the time?'

'To whom?' Rosie demanded. 'You'd already shown me how people were likely to react,' she told him bitterly. 'All I wanted to do was to forget that it had ever happened. So, you see, if you've come here to warn me to keep away from your cousin because he's married you needn't have worried. Like you, he's the last person I want anywhere near me.'

She heard his indrawn breath, but didn't bother to look at him. Suddenly she felt weak and drained, her anger dissipated by her explosion of temper. She felt sick inside and very close to tears, confused and shaken by her own reaction but, most of all, desperately wishing she had not allowed him to provoke her into that verbal outburst.

What good had it done? It was obvious he didn't believe her, but then she had always known that he wouldn't. No, it had been for her own benefit that she had given in to her driven need to tell him the truth, not his.

She started to turn away from him and then stopped as she heard him saying harshly. 'If what you're saying is true——'

If! The anger reignited inside her. She turned her head and looked at him, her mouth curling with a passable imitation of his own disdain.

'*If*? How can it be, when *you* were there? When you saw *everything*. When you have already decided that I was just a cheap little tramp who—'

'I never thought that . . .'

His denial took her by surprise. She stared at him, her expression momentarily unguarded and vulnerable.

'But you . . .'

Grimly Rosie compressed her lips, biting back the words she had been about to say.

'It doesn't matter now,' she told him distantly. 'It was all a long time ago . . .'

'So long ago that you've forgotten all about it, is that it?'

Rosie tried not to shiver as she heard the sarcasm in his voice.

'Of course,' she lied bleakly. 'After all, it's hardly the kind of thing I'd want to remember, is it?'

CHAPTER FOUR

'WHAT do you mean, you're not going? Of course you are. The Simpsons are some of Mum and Dad's oldest friends,' Chrissie said firmly.

Rosie tried to hold on to her temper. Chrissie's pregnancy seemed to be making her bossier than ever, or was it simply that with her outburst to Jake Lucas she had somehow lost a little of her protective coating... her control? Rosie wondered uneasily.

She had noticed a disturbing tendency recently for her emotions to swing far more violently from one extreme to the other. She was constantly tense and on edge, looking over her shoulder, half expecting to find Jake Lucas watching her disapprovingly.

She cringed to think of that awful confrontation she had had with him. *Why* had she told him about Ritchie? What had she hoped to achieve? What had she expected him to do? Apologise... Show regret, remorse, guilt? He hadn't even believed her. He had made that plain enough.

'Rosie...' Guiltily she realised that Chrissie was still talking to her.

'The Simpsons' lunch party... You've got to go... I can't, because we're spending that weekend with Greg's mother.'

'Chrissie——'

'You're *going*,' Chrissie told her firmly. 'Or are you trying to tell me that you've got some hot date? That you're sneaking off to spend the weekend romantically tête-à-tête with someone special?'

Rosie knew when she was beaten. Though she could have pleaded work, she told herself later in the week when she surveyed her desk tiredly.

She had heard nothing from Ian Davies and she knew better than to telephone him, but she had plenty of other work to keep her busy. There had been a spate of burglaries in the area, necessitating house calls on her clients, while she helped them to fill in their claim forms.

It was a time-consuming and non-profit-making task, but she was glad to be kept busy. It kept her mind off Jake Lucas. Or at least it should have done.

Instead of relieving her tension and enabling her to put the past firmly behind her, her furious outburst against his cousin only seemed to have reactivated her pain and despair.

Would she have felt any different if he had believed her?

She frowned. No, of course she wouldn't. She didn't need absolution from him. And anyway,

how could he believe her when doing so would
mean having to admit that he had misjudged her?
No, she didn't need his understanding, his ac-
ceptance. She didn't need *anything* from him, she
told herself fiercely as she bent her head over her
paperwork.

'And so I said to him, well, if you don't tell her,
then I'm going to have to, whether she's your
sister or not... I'm not having her telling me how
to bring up my children...'

'Rosie...I am glad you could make it.'

A little guiltily, Rosie returned Louise
Simpson's warm hug.

'Thank goodness the good weather has held,
although Jim isn't too pleased. He's worried
about people trampling on his precious lawn,'
Louise told Rosie ruefully.

The Simpsons' garden party was an annual
event which normally Rosie enjoyed, but Jake
Lucas had made her feel so hypersensitive that
she felt reluctant to go anywhere, just in case she
might run into either him or his cousin. Not that
Ritchie was likely to be here, she reassured
herself. As far as she could remember the
Simpsons, like her own parents, had never been
particularly friendly with his.

Taking comfort from this reassuring thought,
she followed her hostess out into the sunny
garden, and then froze as almost the first sound

she heard was a child's voice with an unmistakable Australian accent. Panic hit her immediately.

Quickly she turned away, heading in the opposite direction, thankfully merging herself with a group of people around their host.

She stayed there as long as she could, determinedly asking Jim questions about his precious roses long after everyone else's interest had quite obviously faded.

'Better get back to my duties as barman,' Jim told her. 'You haven't got a drink, Rosie. Come with me and I'll get you something.'

She would have preferred to stay where she was, separated from most of the other guests by the rose-hung pergola which was Jim's pride and joy, but Jim already had his hand on her arm and she couldn't refuse.

The bar had been set up on the large, paved area just outside the house. Several large groups of people were congregated around it.

One of the Simpsons' grandsons had taken over as barman, but was now quite obviously pleased to be relieved of his duties and set free to enjoy himself with his friends.

He was a shy boy of around seventeen, who blushed fiercely as Rosie said hello to him.

'The lad's got a bit of a crush on you,' Jim told her with a chuckle as his grandson disappeared. 'Can't say I blame him, mind... if I was twenty years younger...'

Dutifully Rosie smiled, refusing an alcoholic drink and asking for something cool and soft instead.

As she waited for him to pour it for her, she felt a sharp prickle of sensation at the base of her neck, a conviction that someone was watching her. Automatically she responded to it, turning her head to glance over her shoulder, and then she froze.

She was being watched, by Ritchie Lucas. She recognized him immediately, even though, unlike his cousin, *his* physical appearance had changed considerably in the fifteen years since she had last seen him.

At school, Ritchie had been considered good-looking by some of the girls, although personally she had never found his rather beefy blonde-haired looks in the least attractive. To Rosie there had always been something slightly coarse and uncontrolled about the way he looked which, she had subconsciously felt, reflected his personality, so that she had always felt repelled by him. Which was no doubt why he had decided to pick on her as a victim of his callous cruelty.

Now that coarseness was very much more obvious, his skin burned a reddish brown by the Australian sun, his blond hair now more gingerish and very obviously receding. He had put on weight and, to judge from his physical appearance, was not particularly keen on exercise. He was holding a can of beer, and as she looked at him he raised it towards her, acknowledging her presence, grinning at her, ignoring the faintly anxious glance the small dark woman at his side was giving him. Was she his wife? And those two boys with her, were they his sons? Jake Lucas was standing with them, and Rosie shivered, quickly putting down her glass, her drink untouched.

She couldn't stay here now.

'Rosie, are you all right?' she heard Jim asking her in some concern.

'Yes... Yes... I'm fine... It's just that I've remembered a phone-call I should have made...'

She was gabbling, she recognised, her manner causing Jim's concern to increase as she desperately tried to find an excuse to escape.

'Business? Well, feel free to use the phone in the study. You know where it is.'

Her face burning with a mixture of guilt and anxiety, Rosie headed for the house. If she were lucky, she would be able to make her escape without anyone even noticing she had gone. She would have to phone Louise later, of course, and apologise for leaving without saying goodbye to her.

Feverishly planning what she must do, Rosie opened the French window and stepped into the cool darkness of the house.

The noise of the party receded, muted by the glass doors.

Thank goodness she had arrived a little late and had not parked on the drive, where she might have been blocked in by other cars.

She could hear voices in the kitchen, where Louise and her helpers were preparing to serve the buffet.

Feeling almost like a criminal, she held her breath and waited, hoping that no one would come into the sitting-room or see her leaving.

Her heart was beating too fast and unevenly—her body's physical reaction to her mental panic.

She started to walk across the room to the door which led into the hall. It would have been easier to go back outside and walk round the side of the house to the front, where her car was parked, but she was terrified of doing so in case she saw the Lucases again.

She was halfway across the room when she heard the French window open. Immediately she froze.

'Rosie... Not going yet, are you?'

Her heart lurched with fear. Ritchie Lucas. Had he seen her come inside and deliberately followed her, or was it simply a coincidence?

She heard him laugh. She had always disliked his laugh. He had laughed that night when she had tried to make him stop.

'Well, now, you sure have turned out fair dinkum, haven't you? I real beaut... I always did have a yen for you, you know, Rosie...'

He was, if not drunk, then certainly very close to it, Rosie recognised fastidiously as she watched him swaying slightly on his feet. He was sweating heavily, and she could smell the sour, rank scent of his body.

She wanted to turn away from him, to open the door and run, and yet at the same time she was terrified of taking her eyes off him, terrified of breaking that visual contact, clinging to it as though in doing so she was actually somehow physically keeping him at bay.

She was paralysed with fear, she recognised numbly; like an animal trapped in the beam of a car's headlights, she simply could not move, was too *afraid* to move in case in doing so she somehow brought about the very thing she most dreaded.

'Little Rosie... Who knows what might have happened between us if I'd stayed around?'

Sickly Rosie watched as he lurched towards her.

Run...run, a voice inside her screamed frantically, but she was incapable of obeying it.

He had reached her now, was stretching out his hand to touch her, the same hand which had once torn at her clothes, clawed at her skin, forced her hands behind her back while he had laughed at her efforts to escape.

She felt the panic building up inside her, and knew that everything she was feeling was clearly written on her face: the fear, the anxiety, the revulsion...

'You're not wearing a wedding ring... Good on you. Marriage is a mug's game. Gets you landed with a nagging wife and a parcel of brats. You and I could have fun together, Rosie...'

Fun... Rosie felt herself gag as her stomach heaved. He was so close to her now that she couldn't understand how he couldn't see the revulsion on her face.

'Rosie... there you are, darling...'

Her head snapped back in shock as Jake walked into the room.

Darling... Jake had called her darling... What...?

At any other time she might almost have been cynically amused by the way Ritchie gave way to his cousin, stepping back from her as Jake stepped forward, moving aside so that Jake could stand next to her.

'I just came inside to cool down,' she heard Ritchie blustering. 'Didn't realise you and Rosie here had something going, Jake...'

'Naomi's worried about Adam. She thinks he's got a temperature. She wants to go back to the hotel.'

When had Jake taken hold of her arm in that proprietorial, possessive manner? Rosie wondered numbly, as she watched Ritchie turn back to the French window in obedience at his cousin's words.

She had started to tremble, small tremors of shock shaking her body. She tried to control them, knowing that Jake must be able to feel them, but the more she tensed her muscles, the more intense her shuddering became.

She knew what Jake must be thinking, of course, why he had laid claim to a relationship between them that never had and never could exist. No doubt *he* thought she had deliberately encouraged Ritchie to come in here after her... No doubt *he* thought she had deliberately planned the whole thing.

She turned towards him, intending to pull her arm free, but before she could do so the inner door opened and Louise came in, coming to an abrupt and obviously startled halt at the sight of them.

'Jake...Rosie...'

'We were just about to leave, Louise,' Rosie heard him saying. 'Rosie isn't feeling too well... Too much sun...'

Rosie could see the surprise and the speculation in Louise's eyes. Her heart sank. Louise had a kind heart, but she was also a terrible gossip, and Rosie could see quite plainly the interpretation she was putting on finding them together, Jake's hand resting so possessively on her arm, silently laying claim to an intimacy between them which did not in reality exist. And yet she seemed unable to drag herself free as Jake led her towards the open door and through it.

She was still trembling, still physically reacting to what had happened and to her shock, she comforted herself for her lack of will-power and for letting Jake take the initiative.

'You can let go of me now,' she told him stiffly. 'There's no need to march me off the premises like some kind of criminal. Whether you believe it or not, the last thing I want . . . the last person I want to be with is your precious cousin, so if you think I'm——'

'So I saw.'

Rosie stiffened at his curt tone. 'If you're trying to be sarcastic—' she began, but Jake shook his head.

'Now you're the one who's jumping to conclusions,' he told her quietly.

When she stared at him, he explained grimly, 'I saw your face, Rosie. I saw the way you were looking at him. No one, but no one, could fake that kind of reaction.'

Was he actually saying that he believed her? That he *didn't* think she had deliberately enticed Ritchie to follow her? Rosie couldn't believe it. Shock made her sway slightly on her feet, so that Jake's grip on her arm immediately tightened. She heard him curse and then say under his breath, almost pleadingly,

'Don't go and faint on me, Rosie. Not here...'

Faint...? What did he think she was? Rosie wondered belligerently. Of course she wasn't going to faint.

'I *am not* going to faint,' she told him, gritting out each word with separate emphasis.

'I'm glad to her it,' Jake told her cordially. 'But as well as not fainting, do you think you could possibly start walking?'

'You don't have to hold on to me,' Rosie told him fiercely. 'Or to see me off the premises. My car is this way,' she added as Jake ignored her.

'And mine is this way.'

Rosie stared at him and then started to protest.

'I'm not letting you drive,' Jake overruled her. 'Not in the state you're in...'

'What state?' Rosie protested. 'I'm not in any kind of state...'

Abruptly Jake stopped walking, turning her round to face him.

'No?' he said grimly. 'What is it, then? Malaria? That's the only physical cause I know of for someone shaking the way you're doing.'

'I am not shaking,' Rosie denied, but her face had started to burn with reaction and awareness of the fact that she was lying and that he knew it.

'You might as well give up, Rosie,' he told her. 'I am not letting you drive home, even if that means physically carrying you to my car. I wonder if Louise is watching us,' he added speculatively.

Rosie couldn't help it. Immediately she looked anxiously towards the house, and then realised that he was deliberately baiting her.

'Why did you do that?' she demanded shakily.

'Do what?'

She gritted her teeth. 'Why did you tell Louise we were leaving together as if ... as though ...?'

'As though what?' Jake prompted her.

Rosie shook her head, suddenly overcome with reaction. She didn't have the energy to argue with Jake right now, or to demand an explanation of why he had implied to Louise that they were a couple, using that deliberately intimate 'we' ... nor why he had indicated the same thing to Ritchie, either.

'Come on ... let's go ...'

Too drained to argue, she turned mutely to follow him, and then tensed as he slipped his arm round her, pulling her firmly, protectively almost, against his body, as though he knew how weak and vulnerable she was feeling.

Instinct urged her to pull away, but obeying that instinct was too far outside the capabilities of her shock-exhausted muscles.

It was easier simply to stay where she was, to let him guide her towards his parked car.

She was muzzily pondering on why it should feel so comforting to be held so securely against him when she loathed and disliked him so much, when he suddenly stopped walking and cursed briefly under his breath. She lifted her head automatically to look at him, forgetting how close to him she already was.

'It's Ritchie and Naomi,' he told her. 'They've seen us and they're heading this way.'

His breath felt coolly pleasant against her hot skin. He was smiling at her, she recognised with an odd, frantic skipped beat of her heart, his eyes suddenly soft and warm.

'Rosie...'

He had never said her name like that before, and she was startled to discover how different it sounded when he did.

She looked enquiringly at him, her brain, her emotions, her responses still not fully recovered from the fear Ritchie had caused her to feel.

Jake bent his head towards hers; his free hand cupped her face, his skin cool and firm against the nervous heat of hers.

She looked at him questioningly, and then froze as she realised what he was going to do.

It was too late to avert her face and push him away. He was holding her too closely, the arm which had felt so protective and comforting now imprisoning her against him.

Anger took the place of her earlier numb shock. She opened her mouth to demand that he release her.

'Rosie...'

She felt rather than heard him say her name, through the movement of his mouth against her own, her body automatically stiffening in furious reaction at his kiss, her eyes wide open and brilliantly angry; but he ignored the outraged message of her body language, sliding his hand along her jaw, stroking her hair back off her face in a slow, deliberately caressing movement, and all the time he kept on kissing her, moving his mouth lingeringly over her own, caressing her tightly closed lips with gentle deliberation, ignoring the rigid rejection of her body. He was kissing her with a mixture of tenderness and determination that was completely unfamiliar to her, his mouth stroking over her own again and again until it was impossible for her to keep her lips rigid any longer.

She felt them start to tremble, and so, obviously, did he, because the movement of his mouth stilled for a second and lifted from hers, his thumb stroking gently against her lips, applying just enough pressure to make them part slightly.

Rosie glared angrily up at him, letting him know that, while physically he might be able to dominate her, he could not control her mentally.

His eyes were open too. She saw the way they glinted between his lowered lashes as he looked first into her eyes and then down at her mouth, as though to remind her that, despite her mental and emotional dislike and rejection of him, physically she had not been able to do so, and not because of any use of brute force.

He was still looking at her mouth, and an exquisite thrill of horror ran through her as she realised he was going to kiss her again.

'No.' Her denial of him was an anguished, shaken whisper.

'Still not gone yet, Jake?'

'We were just leaving, Ritchie.'

Ritchie!

Rosie could feel the tension gripping her spine, enclosing it with ice-cold fingers of dread. Without being aware of it, she moved closer to Jake, only realising what she was doing when she felt his arm move slightly to accommodate her, and recognised with a tiny dart of disbelief that she had pressed herself so close to him that she could actually feel his heartbeat and the solid strength of the bones and muscles that underlaid his flesh. Was she really seeking protection from her fear of Ritchie with Jake?

'Ritchie, the boys are tired and hungry.'

Rosie could hear the irritation in Ritchie's Australian wife's voice.

'Oh, for God's sake, Naomi, stop nagging, will you?'

The obvious lack of love or respect in Ritchie's voice made Rosie wince. Even without knowing her, Rosie felt sorry for his wife.

She could just imagine how *she* would have felt had she been the recipient of that kind of comment, spoken in front of a stranger from a man who professed to love her, and not just in front of her, a stranger, but in front of their children as well.

She could feel Jake starting to release her, and for one blind, panicky moment she actually wanted to hold on to him, to beg him not to let her go, not while Ritchie was still here, and then she realised that he was reaching round her to open the passenger door of his car for her. Gratefully she got in, her legs unsteady, her face flushing, as she inadvertently caught a glimpse of the leering expression on Ritchie's face.

'Looks like *you* made the right decision, mate,' she heard Ritchie saying to his cousin. 'Seems to me that a fella can have a hell of a lot more fun single than married.'

Rosie saw the nervous, half pleading look his wife gave him and her pity for her increased. She obviously loved him, Rosie acknowledged compassionately. And that love quite obviously made her very vulnerable. Even the two boys seemed slightly nervous of their father and yet, as Rosie watched them walk away, she saw that, young as they were, they were already beginning to adopt their father's bullying and contemptuous attitude towards their mother.

'Poor woman...'

She spoke the words out loud without realising that Jake could hear them.

'Yes,' he agreed tersely as he slid into the driver's seat of his car and closed his door. 'Ritchie treats her abominably, and she's terrified of losing him. Part of the reason she wanted this trip to England was because she hoped that it would give them time alone together as a family. Apparently when they're at home Ritchie prefers to spend his time with his mates.'

The obvious disapproval in his voice made Rosie turn her head to look at him, a small frown pleating her forehead.

In the past she had thought there was little to choose between Ritchie and Jake; they were related by blood and, it seemed, shared a common attitude towards sex. Of the two of them she had disliked Jake more than Ritchie because Jake had been the one to more openly show his contempt of her and to condemn her. Now Jake's reaction to Ritchie's treatment of his wife confused her.

'Naomi is very vulnerable where her relationship with her husband is concerned. Ritchie's obvious interest in you won't help her.'

Rosie stared at him.

'Ritchie's interest in *me*? But——'

'He followed you into the Simpsons' house,' Jake told her coolly. 'And Naomi saw him do so. If I hadn't intervened . . .'

Was *that* why he had held her, kissed her . . . implied that they were lovers . . . not to protect *her* from Ritchie's unwanted attentions, but to protect Ritchie's wife from the pain her husband was causing her?

A pain she hadn't known she was capable of feeling unfolded achingly inside her. Her fingers curled tightly into her palms, nails pressed against her skin to prevent her crying out with the intensity of it. If they hadn't been travelling at some speed she would have been tempted to wrench open the door and fling herself bodily out of the car.

She frowned as she suddenly realised that they weren't travelling in the direction of her home.

'This isn't the way to where I live,' she protested.

'No,' Jake agreed calmly, pausing for a few seconds before adding, 'I'm taking you home with me. We need to talk.'

'To talk?' Rosie stared at him, infuriated by his high-handedness. 'What about?'

The look Jake gave her made her toes curl in nervous self-protection.

'The past . . .' he told her shockingly. 'And the future . . .'

CHAPTER FIVE

THE past! Rosie trembled. What was he planning to do? Grill her so relentlessly that she broke down and retracted the statements she had made about what had really happened with Ritchie?

She had already seen in his face how little he had enjoyed hearing the truth. She knew how much it must have infuriated him, hurt his pride.

And it wasn't just for the sake of his pride that he would want her to retract, either.

She had read into his comments about Ritchie's marriage a none too subtle warning off. Did he *really* think after what she had told him that she would want anything... anything to do with his precious cousin?

He must do, otherwise why the charade about pretending they were a couple? Why that kiss?

That kiss... Her heart started to thump unevenly. Against her will, an unfamiliar mixture of languor and sensuality spilled slowly through her.

She had received other kisses, and yet she could not remember a single one of them affecting her as his had done.

There had been a new dimension to it, an awareness within her of an aching sadness and pain, as though she had suddenly become aware that there could be something in a man's kiss that could stir her so deeply that she was helpless to resist it.

But she *had* to resist it. She had to remember just who Jake Lucas was, and just what the situation between them really was. That hadn't changed just because she had lost her temper and challenged his perception of past events.

He had not followed her into the Simpson's house to protect *her*, as she had initially so naïvely imagined. He had followed her to protect his cousin's marriage.

From her?

She was the last person who wanted to threaten it. As far as she was concerned, she would have much preferred Ritchie to stay where he was in Australia.

At least he seemed to have no memory of what had happened between them. Thank God, but then, remembering how much he had had to drink, it was perhaps not as surprising that he should have forgotten, as she had once thought.

She remembered how terrified she had been all those years ago, dreading hearing that he had been boasting about what had happened, and then how stunned, how disbelieving, when it first began to dawn on her that he couldn't even remember the incident.

She had been glad, of course, but at the same time bitterly resentful that something which should have had such a devastating effect on her and her whole life had had so little effect on his.

For him there had been no guilt, no pain, no suffering, and certainly no remorse.

From what she had seen of him today, she doubted that he was capable of feeling any of those emotions, and for the first time she was thankful that the child she had conceived had been spared the discovery of what his or her father was.

No child should have to suffer that kind of burden; she could see already the effect he was having on his own children.

She shivered suddenly in reaction to what she was thinking. Out of the corner of her eye she saw Jake's head turn in her direction as though he had seen that small physical betrayal.

His terse, 'Almost there,' might almost have indicated concern coming from any other man.

But he had already shown her how little concern he had for her, how little respect for her reputation. To have kissed her like that where anyone could have seen them, to have verbally implied that they were lovers.

These might be the 1990s, couples *might* live together openly and easily without feeling it necessary to marry, believing that their emotional commitment to one another was the only bond they needed. But this was a very small market town where, while mothers and grandmothers might say bravely to their friends that of course they would never dream of pressuring their child to marry simply for the sake of convention and that children were far better off being brought up by two adults who loved them rather than by a married couple who stayed together out of duty, they still admitted privately to their closest friends that, old-fashioned though it made them, they would dearly love to have seen their son or daughter married, preferably before they presented them with their much-loved grandchildren. Rosie knew that, while her parents would never question the way she chose to live her life, they would still, deep in their hearts, be hurt by any gossip linking her name with Jake's in a way that suggested they were lovers with a physically intimate relationship that they had no plans to make permanent.

And then of course there were her clients. Many of them were her own age and some even younger, and she knew they would not be in the least concerned about what she did in her private life. But when she had taken over from her father she had taken on his clients, many of whom had expressed doubts as to her ability to fill her father's shoes, and their attitude, she suspected, would be confirmed once any gossip reached their ears. In their eyes a woman involved in a sexual relationship with a man outside marriage was not his equal, involved in a mutual partnership, but something very different. She would lose status and respect in their eyes . . . And their business as well?

Wearily she closed her eyes, a feeling of helpless despair and resentment washing over her.

Glancing across at her, Jake frowned. Even now, in the intimacy of his car, she still had this ability to withdraw from him, to distance herself from him.

Pain twisted unsparingly inside him. Fifteen— *sixteen* years and nothing had changed. She still had the ability to get under his skin, to touch emotions and needs that no one else had ever come even close to touching.

She hated him, of course. He had always known that. He had seen it in her eyes the night he found her in bed with Ritchie and he had seen it in them on every occasion they had met since.

Until this afternoon.

This afternoon she hadn't looked at him with hatred.

She hadn't looked at him with love, either, he reminded himself.

He had been twenty-three, almost twenty-four, when he'd first realised he loved her, and he had been revolted by that knowledge. She had been just sixteen, still a schoolgirl, a child, and with none of the precocious sexuality of some other girls of her age.

She had been innocent, unknowing . . . uncaring of the effect she was having on him.

He had fought against what he felt with all the power of his intellect and intelligence. He was a man, she was a child; his feelings were a malicious joke played on him by capricious fate, a form of sickness, madness . . . a danger both to him and to her.

They would pass. They had to pass. He could not really be in love with a sixteen-year-old *child* who barely knew he existed, who was closer to his irresponsible cousin in age than himself. All he had to do was to ignore them, to ignore her, and eventually they would go away without harming either of them.

And then he had found her in bed with Ritchie. It had been a neighbour of his aunt and uncle's who had alerted him by telephone to Ritchie's illicit party.

He had arrived there to find the living-room full of drunken teenagers, rock music blaring out so loud he suspected that, sober, their eardrums could not have withstood it.

Unable to find Ritchie, he had automatically gone upstairs, searching his cousin's bedroom first, only alerted to the fact that someone was in his aunt and uncle's by the light shining beneath the door.

Ritchie had been standing beside the bed, fully dressed, when he walked in, but Rosie...

He gripped hold of the steering-wheel as the echoes of the emotions he had felt then surged through him.

She had been lying motionless in the bed, sated by his cousin's lovemaking, he had thought, her clothes in disarray. He couldn't remember actually moving across to the bed, only the look on her face as she turned and saw him.

The savage jealousy which had possessed him had sickened him. If she had wanted so desperately to experiment with sex, what the hell had made her choose his cousin? he had wanted to ask her...

Why hadn't she come to him?

But he had already known the answer, of course. She barely even knew that *he* existed. She probably believed herself to be in love with his cousin and, knowing that Ritchie was shortly leaving the country, that she was unlikely ever to see him again, she had wanted to consummate that love.

Later he was glad that the width of the bed had separated him from Ritchie, otherwise, he suspected, he might not have been able to control the savage murderous impulse which had possessed him.

That he had been jealous—blindingly, achingly, tormentedly jealous—of his cousin had been one thing and bad enough; that he should have physically wanted to punish him, to destroy him almost, because of that jealousy had been another.

He remembered the terrified white-faced look Rosie had given him once she had pulled her clothes on; then he had thought it was that she had recognised what he had been feeling... Now...

He glanced at her. Her eyes were open now, but she was looking away from him, out of the window.

To discover that she had not gone willingly with Ritchie as he had believed, to hear her say that her drink had been deliberately spiked, that his cousin had deliberately planned to hurt and humiliate her... to hear her accuse him of being a part of the reason why she had said nothing... nothing... of what had happened... had made no complaint... no protest...

And this afternoon he had seen in her face confirmation, if he had needed it, of just exactly what she did feel about his cousin.

Why had he been so blind? Why hadn't he realised then...?

Why hadn't he questioned events more deeply? Why, out of his love for her, had he not somehow known what she had chosen to keep hidden from him ... from everyone ...?

When she had needed him most, when she might have *turned* to him as a confidant and a friend, through his own behaviour he had caused her instead to turn away from him, to believe that he despised, condemned her.

Even if he had not loved her he could *never* have done that. She had been a child ... a baby still.

But she had not been a child the day he had gone to see if there had been any repercussions from her relationship with his feckless cousin. Then she had been all woman, cold, distant, remote, while her eyes blazed her defiance and bitterness.

He had thought then that she had somehow blamed him because Ritchie had gone, never coming close to realising what she was really feeling.

But he knew now!

His face hardened as he turned into the private road that led to the small, exclusive development of houses of which his own was one.

Rosie, turning her head to protest again that she had no wish to go home with him nor to listen to anything he might want to say, saw his expression and, shocked by the harshness of it, instead said nothing.

She was still suffering the effects of her run-in with Ritchie, she told herself shakily, as Jake brought his car to a halt on the brick-set drive to his house.

The house, although modern, was built on traditional lines, and like its neighbors was set in a mature wooded landscape, so that the warmth of its brick façade blended comfortably with its green backdrop.

His manners, at least, were very different from his cousin's, Rosie acknowledged, as Jake opened the car door for her and waited courteously for her to get out. Where Ritchie had terrified her with his physical strength and brutality, Jake intimidated her with his watchful distancing of himself from her, with the contempt she had believed he had always felt for her.

She had been conscious of that watchful distance even before he had found her with Ritchie, nervously wondering what it was she had done wrong that made him focus on her like that. She had been in awe of him even before that night, she admitted as she waited for him to unlock his front door.

But she wasn't in awe of him any more. Why *should* she be? And she wasn't going to allow him to intimidate and browbeat her into retracting what she had said about Ritchie.

The house had a good-sized rectangular hallway, immaculately decorated and furnished, but bare of any signs of being lived in.

There was no evidence of any family clutter, no pictures, no flowers, none of the things which, in Rosie's view, went to make a home.

As though he had read her mind, Jake turned his head and said wryly, 'Sterile, isn't it? That's partly because I'm away so much in Greece, and partly because Mrs Lindow, who comes in to clean for me once a week, says she "can't be doing with clutter and flowers making a mess all over the place".'

'I can see her point,' Rosie responded tactfully.

'But you'd have them anyway...mess notwithstanding.'

His comment startled her. She looked up at him, confused by the expression in his eyes, but still unwilling to admit how often she did buy flowers, simply for the pleasure that seeing and smelling them gave her, and then kept them even when their petals had actually started to fall, reluctant to condemn them to the dustbin until the very last one had died.

'I thought we'd be more comfortable in the sitting-room,' she heard Jake saying as he opened one of the doors off the hallway and waited for her to precede him into the room.

Like the hall, it was immaculately decorated and furnished, and like the hall it too was somehow too perfect and sterile, apart from the huge Knole settee in front of the fire.

'It belonged to my grandmother,' Jake told her, watching her study it. 'The designer who organised the décor here for me wanted to throw it out, but I wouldn't let her. Instead we compromised and had it recovered, although in some ways I still prefer the original scuffed velvet...'

'It looks very comfortable,' Rosie responded inanely.

Why was he treating her like this, almost... almost gently, as though he was concerned... afraid for her...?

'It is,' he assured her. 'Try it...'

Without ever having intended to do so, Rosie discovered that she was sitting down on the settee and being dwarfed by the depth and comfort of it.

She heard Jake laugh. 'You look like a little girl on her best behaviour at her grandmother's Sunday tea party,' he told her.

Rosie flushed because that was exactly how she *had* been feeling, uncomfortably aware of the elegance of the settee's silk covering and the fact that her lack of height meant that when she sat back in it her feet could not comfortably reach the ground.

'You can't sit on it like that,' Jake told her. 'Take off your shoes and make yourself comfortable.'

'Oh, no... I couldn't... the fabric...'

'The fabric is only fabric,' Jake told her wryly. 'Possessions are never more important than people. We've got a lot to talk about, Rosie. Would you like something to eat? You missed the buffet at the Simpsons'.'

Rosie shook her head, knowing that, despite the fact that she had eaten nothing since her breakfast, she was far too on edge to do so now.

'A drink then... tea... coffee...?'

Why didn't he just get on with it? Rosie wondered grimly. Was he deliberately playing on her tension, trying to gain the upper hand so that when the crunch came...?

She shook her head.

'Well, I'm going to have something,' she heard him say. 'I shan't be a minute.'

He was barely that, returning just as she had finally decided she couldn't stand the excruciating agony of either sitting with her back ramrod-straight or being unable to bend her knees and had admitted that he was right and that the only way she was going to be able to sit comfortably on the settee was if she removed her shoes and curled up on it.

She was just doing this when he walked in, carrying a bottle of wine and two glasses.

When he filled them both and offered one to her, she shook her head.

'It's only wine,' he told her mildly. Instantly her face was suffused with colour, as she wondered if he was deliberately taunting her with what she had told him about her drink being spiked the night of the party. She couldn't tell him that alcohol was something she never touched. It would make her look too weak and vulnerable.

Instead, reluctantly, she accepted the glass from him. The dark red liquid glowed richly in its plain glass, the only touch of colour in the otherwise neutral room. When she held the glass in her hand, the liquid almost seemed to warm her flesh through it.

She took a sip, surprised to discover how much she liked the warm, fruity taste.

It *was* only wine, she reminded herself, and only one glass, and then, as Jake seated himself at the other end of the settee and turned to face her, she took another nervous sip.

This was it. This was the moment when he challenged her, demanding that she retract what she had said about Ritchie.

'Rosie...the night of the party——'

'I don't care what you say to me...how much pressure you put on me, I'm not going to change what I said,' she told him fiercely. 'What I told you was the truth.'

'Yes, I know...'

His quiet words silenced her. She stared at him and then took a hasty, tense gulp of her wine, grateful for the warmth that spilled through her from it, driving out the icy fingers clutching apprehensively at her muscles.

'You ... You *believe* me ...'

He nodded his head and she felt a huge surge of emotion rush through her. She took another gulp of wine.

'You believe me now, but you wouldn't have believed me then ...'

She saw the look on his face and deep within her something splintered sharply, painfully.

'You wouldn't,' she repeated, denying what she had seen in his eyes.

He bowed his head.

'I *saw* the way you looked ... the disgust ... the contempt ...'

She watched as he twisted his glass in his hands. There was something different about him now, as though ... as though the distance he had always placed between them had somehow gone.

'Those were for me,' he told her in a low voice. 'Not for you. I *did* think you'd gone with Ritchie willingly, though. I thought you believed you were in love with him.'

Rosie shuddered. 'I hated him even then. He was always making fun of me ... taunting me because I didn't ...' She ducked her head uncomfortably.

'Because you were a virgin,' Jake supplied for her.

She couldn't speak, her emotions too raw and painfully close to the surface to allow her to. She nodded instead, taking another sip of wine, hoping it would steady her.

When Jake had brought her here to talk, the last thing she had expected was that they would be having such an extraordinarily intimate conversation ... that he would accept so readily, so easily what she had to say ... that he would say, and mean it, that he believed her.

She felt dizzy with the unexpectedness of it, light-headed ... *light-hearted* almost, as though some huge weight had been lifted from her.

'I felt so ashamed ... so ... so guilty and afraid ...'

'The guilt was Ritchie's.' He paused as he looked at her, and then added in a low voice, 'And the shame mine.'

'It's all a long time ago ... and none of it matters now,' Rosie told him jerkily.

What on earth was she saying? Of *course* it mattered. *She* had never forgotten what had happened ... his disgust ... his contempt ... Only he had just said that they had never been directed at her, but at himself.

'This afternoon ... were you leaving the party because you'd seen Ritchie?'

His abrupt switch from the past to the present caught her off guard.

'Yes,' she admitted. 'I saw you both...' She bit her lip when she realised what she had admitted, and realised from the bleak look he gave her that he had recognised all that she had not said.

'I suppose I deserved that,' he told her. 'I'm sorry if Ritchie upset or frightened you.'

'Well, at least he didn't remember...about the party. He was very drunk that night.'

'But not too drunk to rape you.'

The harshness of his voice startled her, making her body go tense.

'I can understand why you want to protect Naomi,' she told him. 'But I'm no threat to Ritchie's marriage.' She gave him a small, bitter smile. 'Far from it. Your Draconian measures this afternoon to keep me away from him really weren't necessary. He's the last man I'd want in my life, even if he wasn't married...'

She drank her wine quickly.

'I wish you hadn't said what you did in front of him, implying that you and I... If it gets round and people start to gossip... I know it isn't supposed to matter these days, that a woman is as entitled as a man to enjoy her sexuality——' She knew her face was burning, but she was determined to say what she felt must be said.

'But you don't want anyone thinking that you're enjoying *yours* with me, is that what you're trying to say?' he interrupted.

He sounded angry now, more like the Jake she knew, his voice harsh and tense.

'This is a small town,' she told him uncomfortably, 'where people sometimes still make old-fashioned judgements. If it weren't for the business ... I——'

'You'd what?' he demanded. 'Be quite happy for people to think that you and I are lovers?'

He moved towards her and automatically she jerked back from him, her skin burning red beneath the cynicism in his eyes.

'It isn't that,' she protested automatically. 'It isn't you ...'

Helplessly she saw the way he tensed, pouncing on her words.

'Not me,' he repeated softly. She saw him breathe in, awareness glinting in his eyes as he asked her quietly, 'Tell me something, Rosie. How many men ... how many lovers have there been since my cousin raped you?'

To her horror, Rosie felt her whole body start to tremble. She could feel the emotion welling up inside her, the tears clogging her throat, the pain, the panic, the grief, all burning through her in a relentless, unstoppable tide.

'None... None... I didn't... I couldn't...
There wasn't——'

'Rosie... Rosie...'

Almost before she could even blink Jake had
covered the distance between them, taking her
gently in his arms, removing the now empty glass
from her hand, holding her as tenderly and carefully as though she were merely a child...a
baby...

A baby...

The sound of anguish she made was smothered
against his shirt, the tears she hadn't realised she
was crying soaking through the cloth.

She tried to stop, to pull away, to regain control
of herself and her emotions, but Jake wouldn't
let her. Instead he was talking to her, crooning
almost, soft, reassuring words, telling her that it
was all right for her to cry, that it was all right
for her to show him her pain, to share her anguish
and bitterness.

Distantly she heard the small warning voice
that urged her to think, to stop, to cease this act
of idiotic self-betrayal with a man whom she had
always thought of as her enemy.

And yet who better to share what she was
feeling with? Who could understand more...
know more?

'Let it all go, Rosie,' she heard him telling her
gently. 'There's no need to hide it any more. You
have every right to feel pain and anger.'

She realised that he was stroking her hair, the slow movement of his hand not just reassuring her but giving her as well a physical contact with him that some part of her needed.

It was as though by touching her, holding her, talking to her he had almost become a part of her as well as a part of her past.

Words, phrases, emotions, all of them jumbled and turbulent, tumbled from her lips as her control broke. Somehow she was sixteen again and saying all the things she had not been able to say then, expressing all the agony, the guilt, the anger he had caused her to feel.

Once she actually bunched up her fist and pummelled it fiercely against his chest as she relived physically the emotions he had caused her to suffer then, which she had never been able to express.

It didn't occur to her to question *why* the focus of all those emotions should be Jake and not Ritchie. She was not capable of such logical thought, but Jake was.

As he held her and let her emotions pour from her like poison from a lanced wound, he ached with sorrow and guilt for all that she had suffered.

Why had it never occurred to him that she might not have gone willingly with Ritchie? Had it been any other girl but Rosie, he must surely have done, but, in the seething torment of love and jealousy which had seized him, in the blinding belief that she felt for his cousin the desire she would never feel for him, he had not stopped to question her willingness to be there.

Now he realised that the dazed, transfixed stillness of her body had not been caused, as he had so jealously believed, by sensual satisfaction, and was not the aftermath of sexual completion, but on the contrary had been caused by terror and shock and had been her mind's way of escaping from the horror of what had happened to her.

Ritchie hadn't been violent with her, just rough, she had told him when he gently probed her memories. He had used force to overpower her, but the sexual act itself had been over quickly.

Her memory of it was not one of pain but one of shock and shame that she had not somehow guessed what he had intended and been able to stop him.

As he held her and listened to her, he knew that there were no words to express what he was feeling, no relief from the burden of his own guilt.

He couldn't bear to think of what it must have done to her to have kept such a traumatic event to herself, to have felt that there was no one she could confide in, no one who could support and help her, and he could bear it even less knowing that *he* should have been that someone and knowing that, far from being that someone, as he ought to have been, he had actually caused her trauma to increase.

All these years she had kept all that locked away inside her. No one knew better than he how hard it was to lock away any kind of emotional pain, and he considered himself to be an expert on the subject, but somehow *she* had done so, stoically bearing the burden of self-contempt and guilt he had unknowingly given her.

He knew without her having to tell him why there had been no other men in her life, no other man who might have shown her that she had every right to enjoy her sexuality, to take pleasure and joy in it.

He was to blame for that as well.

She was still leaning against him, her body a sweet, warm weight against his own. She was trembling slightly, physically exhausted by the intensity of her emotional turmoil and by reliving the past.

He held her closer, resting his jaw against the top of her head, closing his eyes against the acid burn of his own tears. Not tears for himself—he didn't deserve them—but for her.

He tried not to think about how it could have been . . . how she might have turned to him, how they could have been united by a close bond of friendship and understanding, even if she could never have loved him.

Or maybe even that might have happened as well... Maybe she *might* even have trusted him enough to let him show her what the physical expression of love and desire between two people really should be.

He felt his muscles tense his desire for her— no longer an old hunger, but a sharp, immediate need.

He was old enough now to know that his love for her would never disappear... never change, and he knew enough of his own nature to accept that he was not the kind of man who could ever inflict on someone else, even if they never actually realised it, the role of being second best. Better to remain on his own than do that.

He looked down at the silky russet wing of hair that concealed Rosie's face.

He had hurt her, almost destroyed her. *He,* not Ritchie. It had been *his* reaction, *his* imagined judgement of her... *his* imagined contempt for her that she remembered far more clearly than Ritchie's offence.

She was still trembling, but she had stopped crying... stopped talking.

Exhausted, Rosie lay against Jake's chest. She could feel the heavy, slightly uneven thud of his heartbeat, smell the special personal scent of his body warmth. Instinctively she nestled closer to him, comforted by it.

She had got it wrong, Jake had told her. He had never blamed her, never felt contemptuous of her, and instinctively she had known that he was telling her the truth.

With that knowledge, with that barrier between them removed, had come an overwhelming need to talk about the past, to let the emotions she had kept dammed up inside her spill out.

Now she felt drained and shaky, light-bodied and empty, cleansed of all her corrosive, bitter memories. She lay in his arms, too weak to move, her physical actions still governed by her emotional needs, and the strongest of all those was her need to be close to him, to just lie here and be held by him, safe, protected, comforted, her pain shared and understood.

She closed her eyes sleepily and then opened them reluctantly as Jake said her name, lifting her head to look at him.

He watched her sombrely, and then lifted his hand to gently move her hair off her face, tucking it behind her ear.

Abruptly she remembered the way he had kissed her outside the Simpsons' house, and automatically her glance slid to his mouth, her own lips parting, her lungs expanding as she had to gulp in air.

No one else had ever kissed her like that, made her feel like that, made her forget everything but the sweet intensity of the pleasure curling slowly through her.

Jake bent his head and her heart started to hammer frantically fast.

Was he going to kiss her again? Would it feel the same this time? Would she...?

She touched her lips nervously with her tongue, wetting their dryness, her body tensing as she heard the way he said her name.

Somewhere within her a stern voice warned her that she was being deliberately, dangerously provocative, but she didn't want to listen to it. She wanted him to kiss her, she recognised with a fierce lurch of her heart. She wanted him to hold her, to touch her, to...

Impulsively she reached out and touched him, placing her palm against his jaw. Her breathing quickened with the sudden sensual awareness that flooded her.

'Rosie.'

His voice sounded different as he said her name, thickened, slurred. He turned his head so that his lips touched her palm, caressing it.

A deep shudder went through her, her eyes unwittingly imploring as she reached up towards him.

'Rosie...'

He had intended to protest, to stop her, to explain to her that what was happening to her was just an automatic physical reaction to the emotional turmoil she had just experienced, but instead, as she reached up to him and he felt her breath against his mouth, he ignored what conscience told him he should do and instead stroked her parted lips with his tongue, tasting the richness of the wine she had drunk, feeling the way her mouth and then her whole body quivered openly in response to him, feeling the way his *own* body responded as though galvanized by a surge of sensation he was totally powerless to control.

He heard the soft murmur she made in her throat as he kissed her, felt the soft, vulnerable warmth of her body as she pressed closer to him, and knew that she was not really aware of what she was doing.

His hands touched her face, exploring its delicacy, tracing the shape of her ear, the line of her neck, feeling her shudder violently beneath his touch, and was helpless to prevent himself from deepening his kiss in response to that shudder, tasting her with his tongue, feeling her brief, hesitant shock before she melted against him, opening her mouth fully to him, her hands moving urgently over his back, so obviously impatient with his shirt and the barrier it made between her touch and his flesh that he tugged it out of the way himself, whispering against her mouth how much he wanted her to touch him, and how much he wanted to touch her.

Jake wanted to touch her... Rosie tensed and opened her eyes.

Her hands were pressed flat against the hard, warm flesh of his back, her mouth was soft and swollen from his kiss—the kiss she had silently implored him to give her.

She was trembling violently, aware of so many conflicting emotions that she could scarcely make sense of what she was feeling.

'Touch me,' Jake had told her, and then he had told her as well how much he wanted to touch her.

Now he was holding her, his mouth gently caressing her throat, his hands...

She shuddered as she realised how close his hands were to her breasts. All she had to do was to move very slightly and then he would be touching them.

Would the fingertips which had traced the bones of her face so delicately and sensuously arouse the same pleasure within her if they touched her breasts?

Her body's response to her thoughts made her catch her breath in shock as she felt the fierce pulse of desire that arced through her.

'Rosie... what is it? What's wrong?'

Unable to answer him, she wrapped herself around him, clinging shakily to him, half exalted by what she was feeling and half afraid, but not challenging the extraordinariness of what was happening, or the fact that it should be *this* man who was causing her to feel like this, to experience desire and need, to suddenly know that behind the fear and self-loathing of herself as a woman lay a sensuality that was strong and powerful enough to sweep aside and overcome all the trauma of the past if she let it.

'Rosie...'

She felt Jake hold her, move her, as though he were going to push her gently away from him, but, as his hands slid against the silk of her dress and came into contact with the soft fullness of her breasts, he went very still.

Rosie tensed as well, scarcely daring to move, to breathe...unable to initiate the touch her senses suddenly craved, but longing, aching for him to touch her, to gently remove the barrier of her dress and the silk bra she was wearing beneath it and to caress her breasts with the same care and tenderness with which he had touched her face...to make her feel whole again...clean again, to let her experience a man's desire and to express her own.

And yet, when he did as she had wished, she was suddenly overcome with tension and panic, freezing with a cold fear which could not be dispelled by the warm touch of his hands against her body.

'Rosie . . . it's all right . . . it's all right . . .'

As she heard his voice, heard its reassurance and steadiness, felt him gently release her, the band of fear imprisoning her snapped.

'No . . . please . . . don't stop . . . I want . . .'

The husky, stammered words pierced him like darts of acid fire as Jake watched her . . . loving her . . . wanting her . . . knowing that, in her emotionally wrought state, she *believed* she wanted him . . . knowing that he had no right to take advantage of her confusion, and knowing, as she raised her mouth to his and started to kiss him, that there was no way he was going to be able to resist her . . . to stop . . .

This time when he caressed her breasts the icy coldness of fear had gone, and in its place was a sensation so achingly sensuous and pleasurable that it was Rosie herself who arched her body up towards him, her hands holding his head, her fingers sliding fiercely into his hair, her head dropping back against the damask fabric of the settee as gently, watchfully at first, and then, as he realised that the sensation of his mouth caressing her nipples had not frightened or distressed her, finally giving in to his own passionate need to express his desire for her, he suckled on the hard points of flesh until the needle-sharp darts of sensation that pierced her made her cry out frantically in shocked pleasure.

Drugged with arousal and need, Rosie moved closer to him, and then abruptly she realised what she was doing, and what could happen if she didn't stop.

Jake felt her tension, her withdrawal, and lifted his head to look at her. Her eyes had gone blank with shock and panic.

Had his touch, his caress . . . his love reminded her of Ritchie? Disgust and pain welled up inside him.

'Rosie, please . . .'

He had been about to beg her to forgive him, but Rosie misinterpreted the anguish in his voice and shook her head before he could finish, her eyes still registering the intensity of her emotions.

'No... No... I can't,' she told him. 'I couldn't go through that again...I couldn't endure killing another baby...'

Rosie was barely aware of what she was saying, driven by the weight of her pain and guilt, by the knowledge of how easily she had forgotten the past . . . forgotten what had happened . . . She was sickened by how easy it would have been for her to give in to that ache still pulsing through her and to encourage Jake to make love fully to her.

How *could* she have forgotten what happened with Ritchie . . . the baby she had conceived, the panic and anger she had felt, the guilt and pain when she had lost it, the way that loss had haunted her, shadowing her life?

She was so wrapped up in her own thoughts, so shocked by her own lack of control, by the speed with which her physical desire had over-whelmed everything else, obliterating all that she ought to have felt, that she was completely un-aware of what she had said and what she had revealed until she heard Jake demanding harshly, 'What baby? What are you saying? You told me...'

Realising what she had done, what she had be-trayed, Rosie focused on Jake's face.

The panic that hit her was so intense, so strong, that it was like an icy tide physically engulfing her, swallowing her up and dragging her down into a dark, roaring void.

She came out of it slowly and reluctantly, not wanting to remember what happened, accepting the glass of wine Jake was giving her, distantly aware of his tension, but withdrawing from it.

She felt thirsty, her throat and mouth dry, but when she asked Jake for another glass of wine he frowned slightly, pausing before pouring it for her.

She drank it greedily, needing its warmth, its numbing benevolence, frowning uncertainly as she glanced down at her body and realised that, although her dress was fastened, she wasn't wearing a bra beneath it.

Her nipples pulsed and ached, openly erect beneath the silk.

She suddenly felt overwhelmed by a desire to close her eyes and go to sleep. She yawned and then yawned again, ignoring the sharp urgency in Jake's voice.

'I'm tired,' she told him petulantly. 'I want to go to bed.'

She stood up, her eyes widening in shock as she felt the room sway around her. The two extra glasses of wine she had insisted on having were making her head swim, confusing her thoughts. She yawned again, and closed her eyes.

Jake caught her as she staggered. By the time he had placed her carefully on the settee she was already deeply asleep.

And drunk? On three glasses of wine? A heavy, rich red wine, and she had not had anything to eat, he reminded himself. Add to that the emotional turmoil she had been through, and perhaps it was not surprising that her body and her mind wanted to find escape in sleep.

He ought to take her home, but he couldn't let her go until she had explained that frantic, pleading statement she had made to him.

Had she conceived Ritchie's child? When he had gone to ask her she had told him coldly that she had not conceived. But then, given what he knew now, was it likely that she would have told him anything else?

He bent grimly over her, picking her up.

Luckily Mrs Lindow always kept the spare beds made up. She could spend the night in one of them and then tomorrow they could talk.

Whether she had conceived Ritchie's child or not made no difference to the way he felt about her, to his love for her.

But if she had ... He flinched as he recognised what such an event must have done to her ... on top of all that she was already suffering.

There was no point in trying to wake her now. As he carried her towards the door he paused and looked down into her sleeping face, brushing his mouth gently against hers.

'I love you, Rosie,' he whispered against her lips and, even though he knew she could not have heard him, her mouth seemed to soften into a slight smile.

An omen for the future?

CHAPTER SIX

BECAUSE he was determined there *was* going to be a future for them, Jake acknowledged as he carried her upstairs and carefully laid her down on the bed in the guest bedroom before removing her dress and then going to get one of his shirts to put on her before he pulled the duvet up over her.

She was so deeply asleep that she had barely stirred while he undressed her, and now he stood beside the bed, looking down at her.

It was just as well that she had called a halt to their lovemaking. He knew well enough that the passion and intensity of her response to him had been caused not so much by any personal desire for him, but by the release of all her pent-up emotions.

He would take things slowly with her, give her all the time and space she needed to feel comfortable with him. And if at the end of that she still rejected him... Love could not be forced, he reminded himself, and nor would he want to do so. But if he could keep her close to him, showed her that she could trust him...

He bent and touched her face gently, unable to resist the temptation to do so, and then, straightening his back, he went downstairs.

In the sitting-room Rosie's empty glass was on the floor beside the sofa and with it, almost tucked beneath the sofa, was her bra.

He picked it up and took it upstairs, placing it with her other clothes, remembering the way she had responded to him when he had kissed her breasts, the eager feminine response her body had given him. It wasn't just her physical response he wanted, though. It was her love as well.

Rosie woke up reluctantly, conscious of the dryness of her mouth, of the unfamiliar deepness of her sleep, of the way her head ached.

She moved it slightly on the pillow, frowning as she realised she was not in her own bed.

Immediately she remembered what had happened, her face flushing with mortification as she remembered the way she had cast aside all her normal restraint, all her self-control...the things she had said...the things she had done... Most especially the things she had *done*... Her face burned hotly as she shuddered in mute self-disgust.

It must have been the wine. That and the shock of seeing Ritchie...of discovering that Jake Lucas had not disliked and despised her.

Shock did odd things to people.

Including inciting them to physical desire...
She pushed the thought aside, throwing back the
duvet and then tensing as she realised what she
was wearing...or rather what she wasn't wearing.

Jake must have undressed her before putting
her to bed...undressed her and then wrapped
her in one of his own shirts.

Beneath its fine cotton covering she could see
the flushed areolae of her breasts. They had
looked like that last night after Jake had kissed
them. A tight ball of angry guilt exploded inside
her.

How *could* she have behaved like that, let such
a thing happen—*wanted* such a thing to happen,
and to the extent that, if she had not suddenly
remembered the danger that lay in having sex with
someone without taking precautions against conception, this morning she could well have been
waking up in Jake's bed, not this one... In Jake's
bed...perhaps even in Jake's arms...?

The feeling that swept over her appalled her.
What was happening to her? Twenty-four hours
ago, the last man she could ever have imagined
as her lover had been Jake Lucas, and now...
She didn't want him as a lover now either, she
told herself fiercely. All she wanted to do was to
get up, get dressed and get away from here as
quickly as she possibly could, so that she could
forget that the whole thing had happened.

What had possessed her to break down in front of him like that...to tell him things she had never imagined she would ever share with anyone, to reveal to him emotions, fears, needs so private that she had thought she would never be able to express them to anyone?

And yet strangely it had been easy sharing them with Jake... *He* had made it easy.

Until that moment when she had remembered, realised what she was doing, and she had cried out to him her fear of conceiving another child that she might lose.

She closed her eyes, trying to blot out her memory of the look on his face.

Where was he now? Downstairs waiting for her to put in an appearance...so that he could question her?

Anxiously she looked towards the door and realised that her clothes were on a chair several feet away from the bed, neatly folded with a note propped up against them. The note read,

> Had to go out for an hour. Made fresh coffee at 10.00 am. Aspirins in cupboard if needed.

Fresh coffee... She closed her eyes; she could almost smell it...taste its hot, reviving flavour. As for the aspirins... She grimaced to herself before swinging her feet on to the floor and then wincing as her head pounded painfully.

Her bedroom had its own bathroom, well equipped with everything that she might need, including a new toothbrush. Jake's Mrs Lindow did her job very well, even if she didn't like fresh flowers, Rosie admitted. A hot shower, followed by a final cold rinse that made her skin tingle and the breath lock in her throat, helped to bring her properly round from her deep sleep, a much deeper sleep than she ever seemed to enjoy in her own home.

The silk dress was remarkably uncreased, although Rosie grimaced a little at having to put on clothes she had already worn.

She also felt acutely aware of the fact that the dress was quite obviously not the kind of thing she would have worn for her normal daytime activities. It looked what it was, she decided fretfully as she hurriedly brushed her hair. A 'going somewhere' dress, totally unsuitable for something like yesterday's party, and totally unsuitable for a Monday morning.

If only her car were outside and she could simply drive home. As it was she would have to ring for a taxi and hope that it arrived before Jake did.

The thought of seeing him, of knowing what he was thinking...remembering...made her shudder with self-loathing.

How could she have been so undisciplined, so uncontrolled?

She had been under a lot of stress recently, both from her work and from far more personal emotions. Look at the way she had reacted to Chrissie's announcement about the baby.

The baby... She tensed abruptly, forgetting her desire to escape before Jake returned.

She had told *Jake* about her baby. Or as good as. How *could* she have done that? *Why* had she done it?

The rest of the evening, the fact that she had both wanted and encouraged Jake to make love to her, and the uneasy fear-cum-anger those memories had been causing her suddenly faded to nothing. They were nothing in comparison to her final, her *unbelievable* act of self-betrayal in telling Jake about her baby.

She closed her eyes, remembering the sharp incredulity in his voice as he questioned her, the deep anger in his eyes. She could recall them so clearly that she was forced to marvel at the brain's apparent ability to function independently of its owner's befuddled state.

She *had* to get away from here and fast, she told herself in panic.

She had to get away from Jake and to keep away.

She hurried downstairs and into the kitchen, glancing tensely at the clock on the wall as she looked around for a telephone and a directory.

Half-past ten. She couldn't have woken up much after Jake had gone. She had half an hour before he came back.

If she was lucky she might just be able to get away.

She saw a telephone mounted on the wall, but couldn't see any directory with it. The rich smell of the coffee distracted her, and she was looking longingly towards it, tempted to pour herself some, when without warning the back door opened.

She tensed immediately, her body feeling as though the blood was draining quickly from it as she went cold with shock, only it wasn't Jake who came in, it was his cousin's wife, and with her was an older woman whom Rosie knew vaguely. She was approximately the same age as her own mother, and Rosie seemed to remember that she had been very friendly with Ritchie's parents when they lived locally.

Both women came to an abrupt halt as they saw Rosie. Naomi Lucas spoke first, her thin, tanned face relaxing a little, the smile she gave Rosie genuinely warm and friendly as she apologised quickly for startling her.

'Jake gave me a key and told me to come and go as I pleased. Helen is taking me shopping, and I asked her if we could stop off on the way to warn Jake that Ritchie and the boys are likely to descend on him.' She pulled a slight face and Rosie recognised the tension behind her smile.

'Ritchie isn't very good with children. Jake is much better. Australian men, or at least the more traditional of them, don't always take easily to the responsibilities of parenthood.'

It was on the tip of Rosie's tongue to point out that Ritchie was not an Australian but British, but she caught back the words, reminding herself that Naomi was Ritchie's wife and obviously loved him, while she disliked him and felt antagonistic towards him.

The friendliness of Naomi's manner surprised her a little, as the previous day she had felt that the other woman was regarding her with some hostility.

Feeling both uncomfortable and vulnerable, and all too aware of the speculative glances Naomi's companion was giving her, Rosie was just wondering how on earth she could make some rational explanation for her presence here in Jake's kitchen when Naomi smiled at her again and said warmly, 'I hadn't realised yesterday that you and Jake were together... I'm sorry if I seemed a bit offhand. I guess Jake would have got round to introducing us officially sooner or later. We've only just arrived here, after all. Is Jake going to be long?'

Rosie could neither move nor speak. The shock of what Naomi had just said had robbed her of the ability to do either.

She had known yesterday, of course, that Jake's behaviour was bound to give rise to some speculation and gossip, but this morning she had told herself firmly that if she ignored it and just pretended nothing had happened then everyone else was bound to follow suit. But now, with those casual, friendly words, Naomi had unsuspectingly, but very, very definitely, made that completely impossible.

She could see Helen Steadings—she had just managed to recall the woman's name—looking speculatively at her and taking in the significance of the silk dress she had been wearing yesterday afternoon and was still wearing this morning, and Rosie felt her face start to burn painfully and betrayingly.

She might just as well have stood in the town square and told everyone that she had spent the night with Jake, she recognised bleakly as she saw Helen Steadings's speculation turn to certainty.

To Naomi it might not be important that she and Jake had spent the night together, and Rosie knew rationally that these days there was nothing unusual in a couple of her and Jake's age having a sexual relationship if they chose to do so, but Helen Steadings knew, as well as Rosie did herself, that Rosie was simply not in the habit of having that kind of relationship. Her heart sank as she recognised the interested curiosity in Helen Steadings's scrutiny of her. It was not even as though she could come up with any logical or reasonable excuse to explain away her presence in Jake's house in Jake's absence, something strong enough to refute Naomi's innocent assumption that they were established lovers, and anyway, Rosie acknowledged sickly, it was too late for that now.

The time for that had been immediately after Naomi had started to speak, not now, far too many telling seconds later.

'Well, I guess there's no need for us to wait for Jake now,' Naomi was saying cheerfully. 'You must both come over to the hotel and have dinner with us. Jake can——'

'Jake can what?'

Rosie's stomach muscles cramped involuntarily as she heard Jake's voice and realised that she had been so caught up in her dismay that she hadn't heard him returning.

Neither, it seemed, had Naomi, because she turned round quickly, smiling at him, exclaiming, 'Jake...I didn't hear you come in...I was just saying to Rosie that the two of you must come and have dinner with us...I called to warn you that Ritchie is in charge of the boys and that they might all descend on you.'

It was instinct rather than habit that made Rosie step back into the shadow of the kitchen's large dresser. If she could have disappeared altogether she would have been only too happy to do so, she acknowledged miserably.

'Why didn't you tell us about Rosie?' she heard Naomi demanding teasingly. 'I had no idea until yesterday that the two of you...'

Rosie thought she had successfully stifled the small moan of protest she could feel rising in her throat, but Jake had obviously heard it because he lifted his head and stared straight at her.

His eyes looked different this morning, silver rather than grey, alive with a warmth she had never seen in them before... It must be for Naomi, she decided wretchedly. It certainly couldn't have been caused by her. Her stomach trembled nauseously as she remembered the previous evening.

How on earth, *why* on earth had she got herself involved in such an appalling situation? Thank God her parents were away. Hopefully the gossip might have died down before they returned. Chrissie would hear it, though—Chrissie! What on earth was she going to say to her sister?

Chrissie was bound to demand to know what was going on, why *she* had not been told anything about Rosie's supposed relationship with Jake Lucas. Outwardly she might not show it, but inwardly she would be hurt by what she would perceive as Rosie's secretiveness.

And yet Rosie knew that she could *not* tell her the truth, that not even to her own sister could she betray her own lack of self-control, of self-respect.

It had been Chrissie who, when she was a teenager, had sternly pointed out to her what boys thought about girls who had no respect for themselves. An old-fashioned view now, perhaps, but one which Rosie suspected her sister still held.

What on earth was she going to say, to do...? She could feel the panic starting to build up inside her. Perhaps she could appeal to Helen Steadings...ask her to forget what she had seen...heard; perhaps...

'We haven't told *anyone* yet, have we, darling? Not officially.'

Jake's voice broke into her frantic thoughts. He was coming towards her, his smile as tender as his voice.

'Selfishly we wanted to keep the way we feel about one another to ourselves for a little while longer. We haven't even told Rosie's family yet...'

Immediately Naomi pounced, clapping her hands together in excitement.

'Jake, you mean that you and Rosie...? When do you intend to get married? Will it be while we're here? What a pity the boys aren't younger, they could have been pages...'

Rosie made a strangled sound in her throat. Jake was standing in front of her, shielding her from sight, but he could see her and she could see him. She knew he must be able to see the panic in her eyes, and the shamed guilt.

Why on earth had Jake had to bring her back here with him last night? If he had simply taken her straight home, none of this would have happened.

'Is there going to be an official engagement party?' she heard Naomi asking. 'Or——'

Jake turned round. 'That's for Rosie to decide,' she heard him saying easily. 'As for a wedding——' he turned back to Rosie, his eyes sombre as he reached out and touched her face gently, tenderly, causing her to stare at him in dumb bemusement '—naturally, Rosie wants to wait until her parents get back for that, don't you, my love?'

His love... Rosie swallowed. What on earth was he doing... saying...? Didn't he realise that with every word he uttered he was making things a hundred, a thousand times worse, not just for her, but for both of them?

Where initially she had been pleased, grateful almost, to him for giving her presence in his home, in his bed, a covering cloak for semi-respectability, now she was appalled that he could have let things go so far.

To protect her... to protect both of them by concealing the fact that her intimacy with him had been caused by her own lack of self-control, that it had in fact been a potentially tawdry and merely sexual encounter, was one thing; to go over the top in the way he had just done and to imply that they were making plans and as good as engaged...

And that was what he *had* done. She could hear Naomi asking excitedly if she had as yet chosen her ring, and exclaiming to Helen Steadings that she was thrilled to bits with Jake's wonderful news.

It isn't true, Rosie wanted to tell them, none of it's true. But just as though Jake sensed the impulse exploding inside her his thumb brushed lightly against her mouth as though to silence her.

It did more than that... much, much more. Her senses and emotions, presumably still heightened by tension and stress, reacted immediately to his touch, flooding her with sensuality and awareness, reminding her of how she had felt the previous evening when he had touched her... kissed her. She could actually feel her body starting to tremble, her self-control starting to slide. A feeling of helpless anguish filled her, anger against herself and against Jake too, humiliation because of the way she felt and because she was sure he must know what was happening to her as well.

Ever since she had woken up she had been telling herself that what had happened last night could never have done so if she hadn't been upset in the first place, if she hadn't drunk all that wine, more than enough to have a disastrous effect on someone who normally never touched alcohol at all. That had been her protection, her escape, her defence against what had happened, and now with one light touch Jake had destroyed those protective barriers, showing her that physically she was as vulnerable to him, as responsive to his touch sober as she had been drunk.

She heard Helen Steadings saying something about them having to go. Jake moved away from her, escorting the two other women to the door, but not before Naomi had hugged her briefly and told her how pleased she was about their news.

It wasn't Naomi's fault, Rosie reminded herself while Jake was walking them to their car. Naomi wasn't the one who had drunk three glasses of wine and then proceeded to pour her heart out to Jake... to cling to him and make those small moaning sounds of pleasure which still echoed hauntingly in Rosie's own ears.

No, but she *had* come round here this morning and she *had* brought Helen Steadings with her and, but for that, Rosie might just have been able to escape without anyone knowing that she had spent the night here under Jake's roof.

All right, so there *had* been that small incident at the party but, alarmed as that had made her at the time, it had been nothing compared to this.

When Jake walked back into the kitchen she was still standing where he had left her. The look on her face made him ache to take hold of her and comfort her, to tell her that everything was going to be all right. Instead he simply asked calmly, 'Would you like some coffee?'

Coffee. Rosie stared at him. How could he stand there so calmly offering her coffee after what had happened? Anger boiled up inside her, her self-control snapping.

'How *could* you do that?' she demanded shakily. 'How *could* you let them think that you and I . . . that . . . we are about to get engaged . . . ? Have you any idea what you've done?'

Rosie could hear her own voice rising, sharpening with hysteria.

Abruptly she stopped speaking. She must not allow herself to get out of control; her own panic increased her tension, and with it her awareness of her vulnerability.

'What would you have preferred me to do?' Jake asked her quietly. 'Allowed Helen Steadings to continue to think, as she so obviously was doing, that you and I were indulging in a hole-and-corner sexual fling? Is that really how you want to be gossiped about?'

'Why should *you* care how people gossip about *me*?' Rosie demanded tautly. 'You're a man; no one will think the worse of you for having a relationship that's merely sexual——'

'*I* would,' Jake contradicted her flatly, the vehemence in his voice startling her into looking straight at him. His eyes had lost that silver warmth they had had earlier, she recognised, and were once again the cold metallic grey she remembered. 'I'm not some sexual stud intent on chalking up a tally of conquests,' he told her in fierce disgust. 'My reputation is every bit as important to me as yours is to you, Rosie. *I* don't want to be judged as sexually promiscuous any more than you do. Having people talking behind my back speculating about what kind of relationship we have is every bit as repugnant to me as it is to you.'

Rosie shivered as she listened to him. *How* did he know so much about her, about the way she felt, the way she reacted? How could he know those things when everything she had done last night must surely have given him completely the opposite impression?

'But to let them think we were virtually engaged . . . discussing marriage . . .'

Jake turned away from her, removing the filter from the coffee machine. His voice was slightly muffled as he told her, 'Engagements can always be broken, you know... relationships allowed to quietly fade...'

Relationships?

'We don't *have* a relationship,' she protested frantically, and then as Jake turned round and looked at her she felt herself flushing to the roots of her hair.

There was no need for him to point out that last night she had virtually offered herself to him, inviting an intimacy she had never come anywhere near wanting to share with anyone else.

'We can't do this,' she told him in panic. '*I* can't do it...'

She turned away from him, feeling her body start to shake with tension.

Logic told her that what she really ought to do now was to talk the whole thing out with him so that they could find some sensible and workable solution to the situation, but emotionally she knew that she just wasn't strong enough to do so.

She wanted to go home, to be on her own, to shut herself away from everyone and everything to give herself time to build up her defences, and to feel whole and safe again.

Just being here with Jake made it impossible for her to do any of those things. He undermined and unnerved her even without trying. She couldn't even look at him without remembering last night, without remembering the scent and taste of his skin, the feel of his hands on her body.

'I want to go home.'

She sounded more like a petulant, frightened child than a mature adult, she recognised bitterly as her taut demand filled the tense silence.

'If I could use your phone, I'll ring for a taxi.'

There, that sounded better, more positive, more adult. More the persona she was used to projecting on the outside world. The inner person, the vulnerable, frightened person she had betrayed so stupidly to Jake last night, was one she always kept hidden, known only to herself, but now Jake knew about that person as well. She wanted to take back that knowledge, to wipe his memory free of it.

'There's no need for that. I'll drive you——'

'No.'

Her denial was sharp and instant, and laced with panic, she recognised.

'I . . . I have to call and pick up my car.'

'There's no need. I did that this morning.'

Rosie stared at him. 'You... But... Did anyone see you?' she asked him quickly.

'It's too late to worry about that now, Rosie,' he reminded her wryly. 'The horse has already bolted.'

CHAPTER SEVEN

EXPERIENCE... life had taught Rosie that the best way, the *only* way for her to deal with emotions and situations she couldn't control was simply to blot them out altogether, not so much to pretend that they hadn't happened, but rather to refuse to allow herself to admit that they had; and this was precisely what she was doing now, or at least what she was trying to do, she admitted as her concentration wavered from the pile of work on her desk and her thoughts slid helplessly towards Jake.

It was almost twenty-four hours since she had last seen him now. Twenty-four hours since he had driven her home and seen her courteously and safely inside her front door. Twenty-four hours... more now, since he had publicly linked them together as a couple.

Every time her telephone rang she tensed, half afraid to answer it, but on each occasion the caller had been ringing with a legitimate business enquiry.

She had barely slept the previous night, too afraid to close her eyes in case she started thinking about Jake... remembering... But what was there

to think about, after all? Just a few sorry minutes
of indiscretion and stupidity, that was all, but,
no matter how often she tried to tell herself that
her behaviour had merely been the result of too
much tension and too much to drink, that didn't
stop her from being filled with shame and anguish
over what she had done and from being afraid
that, in some way, having once behaved so...so
wantonly, she was somehow vulnerable to doing
so again.

Again... No...she wouldn't do that...
couldn't, surely? She was in such a state of panic
that the telephone had rung several times before
she heard it. She reached automatically for the
receiver, speaking into it and then only just man-
aging to mask her surprise when she realised that
it was Ian Davies on the other end of the line.

He had been reading through her proposals and
projections, he told her, and had been very impressed by them. He wanted to arrange another
meeting so that they could discuss them at greater
length.

Quickly Rosie opened her diary, agreeing the
date he was suggesting.

'Oh, and by the way we must have dinner
together one evening; the four of us—you and
Jake and Anne and myself.'

As she replaced the receiver, Rosie couldn't
help wondering angrily if Ian Davies's apparent

change of heart towards her had anything to do with the gossip he had obviously heard about Jake and herself.

And if it had, what would his reaction have been had the gossip labelled her as Jake's casual sexual partner as opposed to his 'fiancée'?

It was all wrong that, as a woman, her professional and business capabilities and expertise should be judged on her personal life, but she had known from the moment she realised that her name was going to be linked with Jake's that there *were* people locally who would take that kind of attitude, she reminded herself bitterly.

She stared at the telephone, half wishing that she had told Ian Davies that she didn't want his business, her female pride outraged by his old-fashioned attitude; but if she was to maintain her father's success she could not afford to indulge in that kind of sentimental self-indulgence, she reminded herself hardily. No.

After all, no man would do so. But then no man was ever likely to suffer the patronising attitude she had just come up against, she told herself fiercely. She wanted to be judged professionally on her own merits, not on some reflected glow from the business acumen of someone else—a *male* someone else.

She was still seething inwardly at the injustice of the attitude of Ian Davies and of all men like him when Chrissie burst into her office.

'Rosie, how could you?' she began bitterly, launching her angry attack before Rosie could even greet her, never mind ask her how her weekend had gone. 'Have you any idea of what an idiot you've made me look? When Sara Lewis told me the news this morning, I didn't have the faintest idea what she was talking about, and of course *she* realised straight away. She would... And now it will be all over town that you and Jake——'

Rosie froze.

'That Jake and I what?' she interrupted Chrissie huskily.

Had Chrissie heard that she and Jake had spent the night together? Were people gossiping about her, speculating on just how long she and Jake had been having a secret sexual relationship before they were found out... before she was found out? After all, no one was going to condemn Jake for having sex with her, were they? No, their condemnation, their criticism, they would all be reserved for her, Rosie acknowledged miserably.

Chrissie was glaring at her, her face still flushed with anger. It was so unusual for Rosie to take the initiative and interrupt her that she had actually silenced her, but not for long, Rosie recognised, her heart sinking.

'That you and Jake are planning to get married, of course,' Chrissie told her tartly. 'What else?'

The relief that filled her was so intense that it was several seconds before Rosie recognised its shaming significance. If people were going to gossip about her, she was obviously so much a product of her small-town upbringing that she actually *preferred* to hide behind the deceit Jake had concocted to conceal the truth rather than to let them know what had really happened. Was she really so hypocritical?

If there had just been herself to consider it would be different but there was Chrissie and her family. Chrissie's children were just at an age where they would be vulnerable to any kind of adverse gossip about members of their family, and then there were her parents, and the business . . .

'Why on *earth* didn't you *say* something . . . tell me . . .' Chrissie was demanding furiously. 'Honestly, Rosie, I don't understand you . . . I mean, it isn't as though the two of you were indulging in some kind of sordid, clandestine sexual fling. *That* I could understand your wanting to keep secret.'

Rosie flinched, wishing she could shut out her sister's bluntly corrosive comments. Chrissie had no idea of the effect of what she was saying, of course. Why should she have?

'Have you any idea of how much of a fool you've made me look? My own sister is on the verge of getting engaged, and I don't know a thing about it...

'As it is, I'm sure that Sara knew quite well that I was lying when I told her we'd decided to keep the whole thing quiet because you and Jake hadn't decided on a final date for the wedding as yet.

'Rosie...*why* didn't you tell me? I had no idea you were even seeing Jake, never mind... To come home and find out that everyone else but me does know...and to have that cousin-in-law of his going on and on about what a pity it is that her two boys are too old to be pages, and how she'll have to buy her outfit over here because of the difference in seasons... Honestly, Rosie, I just don't understand you. To tell someone who's a virtual stranger before you'd said anything to me...especially when the parents are away.'

To her dismay Rosie realised that, behind her anger, Chrissie was very genuinely upset and close to tears. Wretchedly guilty at having upset her, especially so early in her pregnancy, she said the first thing which came into her head to try and soothe her.

'It isn't definite that Jake and I *will* get engaged. The whole thing's been exaggerated. If

there had been anything to tell you, Chrissie, I
would have done so——'

'What do you mean it isn't definite?' Chrissie
interrupted her grimly.

As she looked into her sister's face, Rosie recognised that her attempt to soothe her had had
almost the opposite effect and that, if anything,
Chrissie looked angrier than ever.

'You spent the night with him, Rosie. Oh, yes,
I heard all about *that*,' she added scathingly. 'Of
course, I know you're an adult and old enough
to make your own decisions, but with Allison
coming up to such a vulnerable age, I hope she
isn't going to start thinking she can follow your
example... It was bad enough finding out from
someone else about your engagement, but if
you're trying to tell me that——'

Suddenly Rosie had had enough.

'That what? That Jake and I made love... had
sex? Why shouldn't we? As you've just pointed
out, we *are* adults. I'm your *sister*, Chrissie, not
your daughter, and if people in this town haven't
got anything better to do than to gossip about
something which is none of their business... none
of anyone's business apart from Jake's and
mine...'

She heard the outraged hiss that Chrissie gave,
but ignored it, all the tension, fear and misery
she had kept dammed up boiling up inside her
and refusing to be contained.

'Why *should* I have to tell you or anyone else what I'm planning to do? Did *you* tell me that you weren't using any form of birth control and might conceive another child...'

This time she did respond to Chrissie's outraged gasp, her temper leaving her as quickly as it had come, leaving behind it a cold feeling in the pit of her stomach and a shakiness to her muscles, plus the miserable sense of having been both unfair and unkind to her sister.

She saw that Chrissie obviously thought so as well, because she was as pale as she had been flushed before.

'I can see there's no point in trying to talk to you while you're in this kind of mood,' Chrissie told her as she turned towards the door. She paused and looked at Rosie. 'I'm sorry if you think I'm prying,' she added stiffly.

She had gone before Rosie could open her mouth to stop her and to apologise for her own behaviour.

Chrissie had been wrong to burst into her office demanding explanations, but she had had every right to feel hurt at what she saw as being deliberately excluded from something which was apparently common knowledge to others.

There was no chance of her being able to tell her sister the truth, though, Rosie recognised. Not after Chrissie's outburst about the effect of her behaviour on Allison's moral outlook.

That too had been an unfair comment, but this unexpected pregnancy had put Chrissie on edge, making her far more dramatically emotional than usual.

Pregnancy *had* that effect on some women, especially in the early months. Rosie remembered how she had felt ... How ...

She closed her eyes, balling her hands into tight, tense fists. Hadn't she got enough misery to think about without adding that?

She would *have* to find some way of placating Chrissie, of course. But how? The last thing she wanted was Chrissie taking an authoritative and stage-managing role in her supposed engagement and marriage plans. She wouldn't put it past her sister to actually almost steamroller her and Jake into marriage. It was just as well that their parents were away and not due to return for several months. Not even Chrissie would expect her to get married in their absence; by the time they did return, they could have brought their relationship to a discreet end as Jake had suggested.

None of this would have happened if Jake hadn't laid such public and unnecessary claim to her, she told herself wrathfully ten minutes later as she paced her office, trying to think up some way to appease Chrissie without inflaming the situation any further. Now if she had not drunk those three fateful glasses of wine ... Angrily she turned on her heel and stared blankly out of the window.

It was as much Jake's fault as it was hers, she told herself stubbornly. More, because he had been the one who had first pretended . . .

A few words . . . a kiss; *that* could have been explained away. Her presence in his house so early on a Monday morning, wearing the same dress she had been seen out in the previous day . . . that had only one logical explanation. Only one explanation people would want to believe.

She would *have* to find some way of making amends to Chrissie; a small, worried frown creased her forehead. She hated being at odds with her sister, who, she knew, beneath her outer bossiness did genuinely love her and had been hurt.

She picked up the telephone receiver and dialled her sister's number, sighing under her breath when there was no response.

She would just have to go round there this evening, and in the meantime she would just try to find some excuse that Chrissie would find acceptable.

An hour later, when she was still having trouble concentrating fully on her work, she acknowledged that if she was to get through her day's workload she would now have to forgo lunch. The pad on which she had scribbled down Ian Davies's name caught her eye. Was it really less than a week ago that she would have been over-joyed to learn that he was offering her his business?

She still would have been overjoyed if she had been offered it for the right reasons, she re-minded herself.

The phone rang, breaking her concentration. She reached for the receiver, freezing as she heard Jake's voice.

'I'm at home,' he told her. 'We need to talk. Could you call round here?'

'Now?' Rosie questioned angrily. Her heart was beating far too fast and she suddenly felt slightly dizzy and sick. The last person she wanted to see was Jake, but as she tried to concentrate on thinking up an excuse that would not betray her vulnerability she heard him saying quietly,

'Yes... If you could... It *is* rather important...'

What was rather important? Rosie wanted to demand, but he had already replaced the re-ceiver, quite obviously taking her agreement for granted.

As she stepped into the reception area, she wondered if she was being oversensitive in thinking that Jane, who worked for her, was looking at her rather speculatively.

'I... I have to go out for a while,' she told her, conscious of the fact that her face was burning hotly and that she felt as guilty as a small child telling a fib.

The first thing she saw when she pulled up outside Jake's house was Chrissie's car. She stared at it, her heart sinking, and then reluctantly opened her own car door.

Jake must have been watching for her, because he had opened the front door and was coming towards her almost as soon as she had locked her car.

He was wearing a suit, dark grey, with an immaculate white cotton shirt and a discreet silk tie. He didn't look like the man who had held her and touched her, who had stroked her and kissed her...who had made her body ache and burn. This was the old Jake—the formidable, austere, disapproving Jake who had haunted her.

She stood still, panic and dread flaring inside her, her expression unknowingly betraying what she was feeling so that Jake cursed under his breath.

He had promised himself that he would take things slowly, that he would use this opportunity fate had so unexpectedly given him to put their relationship on a fresh footing. He had told himself that now that he knew the reasons why she had always held him at a distance and rebuffed him he could surely find a way of slowly overcoming them.

Logically he knew that just because he now knew what had caused her aversion to him that did not mean that anything would change, but emotionally his heart had cried out that surely it was impossible to love someone so much and for so long and for that love not to be returned. Sexually she was responsive to him. To him... Not to his cousin, not to anyone else... To him.

Now, as he saw the panic in her eyes and sensed how tempted she was to turn round and run, he reached out to her, shocked by the icy-cold tension of her skin.

'Your sister's here,' he told her.

'Chrissie...'

She had flinched when he touched her, but she hadn't pulled away.

'She arrived in a bit of a state,' he added, watching her. 'I gather the two of you had a bit of an upset...'

The dazed, frantic look was leaving her eyes now, the pupil no longer dilating quite so painfully.

Why was it that, when she *knew* it was the most dangerous thing she could allow, she was letting him touch her... hold her? Rosie wondered bleakly. It wasn't just because the touch of his hand on her arm was warming, soothing. Soothing... That wasn't what the rapid acceleration of her heartbeat was telling her.

'You're cold. Let's go inside.'

Numbly she let him take charge, calmly ushering her inside.

She tensed on the threshold to the sitting-room, her eyes going instinctively and betrayingly to the Knole settee.

If Jake was aware of what she was doing, he gave no sign of it. Instead he was smiling at Chrissie, who was sitting on the edge of one of the fireside chairs, her expression strained and nervous.

'Rosie...I'm sorry about...about what happened earlier,' Chrissie began, before Rosie could speak.

'Jake...Jake has explained to me that he had asked you not to say anything until he'd completed the negotiations for selling his share of the marina business. He told me that you'd wanted to tell me, and that you had intended to do so this last weekend.' She made a wry face. 'I suppose I didn't help, bursting out with our news about the baby the other Friday, not giving you a chance to get a word in edgeways. I suppose I did rather over-react this morning. I should have realised you wouldn't deliberately keep something like this from me. It was just...just that I felt so hurt hearing it from someone else...'

'I know,' Rosie told her contritely. The pain gripping her stomach muscles was beginning to ease. She had Jake to thank for Chrissie's calmer mood, she recognised, and for shouldering the blame for keeping their 'news' from her.

'I *am* pleased for you...of course,' Chrissie continued, 'and I *do* understand why you both felt that you had to make your relationship public in view of what happened on Sunday. As Jake said, the last thing any of us would want is for people to start speculating that the two of you might be having some sordid secret affair.'

She got up and walked across to Rosie, hugging her.

'I'm sorry, Rosie,' she told her in a muffled voice. 'I was rotten to you earlier. I came round here intending to tell Jake what I thought of the pair of you, and instead he made me see how difficult I was making things for you...'

Rosie didn't say anything. She couldn't. Every word Chrissie said to her was increasing her guilt tenfold.

It was left to Jake to take hold of her hand and draw her closer to him, close enough for him to place his arm around her waist, holding her against the warmth of his body, causing nervous, fluttery sensations of quicksilver apprehension to race through her.

'We do understand, don't we, darling?'

As he spoke he turned to look at her, his free hand gently brushing her hair back off her face and lingering against her skin just long enough to make her nerve-endings prickle sensitively and her mouth feel as though it had started to swell slightly, as she remembered how she had felt when he kissed her.

He was looking at her mouth now, she recognised. Looking at it . . . and lowering his head as though . . . He couldn't possibly be going to kiss her, surely? Not in front of Chrissie? Not when they both knew . . . ?

'Rosie . . .'

Her mouth quivered as she felt the warmth of his breath against her sensitive skin. Her eyes were already closing, her body turning in towards his, her hands pressed flat against his chest.

He kissed her gently, lingeringly, and the ache of need that pulsed inside her was so keen and sharp that for an instant she almost forgot that Chrissie *was* there, so great was her need to cling to him and return his kiss, to feel his mouth harden with passion, to feel his body . . .

Abruptly she surfaced from her dangerous fantasy, her face flushed with guilty heat.

Mercifully Jake wasn't watching her, and had turned away from her as he released her, but Chrissie was. And, as they looked at one another, Rosie recognised the message in her sister's eyes.

Chrissie knew that she loved him. She *loved* him! The shock seemed to go on forever, seeping into her slowly, briefly numbing her, and then receding, allowing the space it had left behind to be filled with the raw acid burn of her terrified panic.

'Look, I'd better be going,' she heard Chrissie saying but, as she turned automatically to go with her, Jake stopped her.

'I'll see you out,' he told Chrissie.

'I'm sorry I made such a fuss,' Chrissie apologised to her, giving her another hug. 'This baby is playing havoc with my hormones, I'm afraid... Still,' she grinned at Jake, 'if you and Rosie don't waste too much time, he or she could have a cousin to grow up with.'

She wanted to leave, to get away right now, to go somewhere where she could be alone to examine her pain in private... somewhere where she could lock herself away so no one else could see or suspect what was happening to her.

How *could* she be in love with Jake? Rosie asked herself helplessly as she watched him escort Chrissie to her car and knew that it was impossible for her to follow her.

She and Jake were supposed to be in love; *she* was in love... what woman in love would rush away from her lover, refusing the opportunity to share a few minutes' privacy with him? Especially after the way Jake had kissed her... a kiss which Chrissie had very obviously interpreted as a restrained expression of his desire for her.

But *she* didn't want Jake to desire her. She didn't want him to touch her, kiss her, arouse her, expose her to the newly discovered dangers of her love for him.

No wonder he made her feel so on edge, so nervous... Had some part of her known all along... felt all along? Was *that* why she had reacted so intensely to him all those years ago? Had something in her recognised it even then?

She heard Chrissie drive away.

Panic exploded inside her.

She didn't want to be on her own here with Jake.

But it was too late now to try to escape. She heard the front door open and then close again, and her fear increased.

CHAPTER EIGHT

'I DIDN'T realise your sister was expecting another child.'

Rosie didn't look round as she heard Jake come into the room—she didn't dare; but as she heard the quiet calmness of his voice her panic was stoked by a sudden flare of anger.

He was taking things so calmly, so easily. Didn't he have *any* idea of what it was doing to her... of what *he* was doing to her?

As he studied her rigid back, Jake's heart sank. She didn't want to be here with him, he knew that. It hurt him, knowing how much she wanted to get away from him, but he clamped down on his desire to make things easier for her, to open the door and let her walk through it.

Deep inside him there was a growing awareness that there was another and far more important door that was locked and barred, holding her imprisoned behind it.

Was he deluding himself in believing that he might be able to help her find its key and set herself free?

There was such a lot of pain locked up inside her, such a burden of anguish and unhappiness.

He had heard it in her voice the night she had told him she had conceived Ritchie's child, had seen it in her eyes just now when Chrissie had mentioned her own pregnancy.

He was a man and could only guess at how it felt to be a woman; he was afraid of being clumsy and careless, adding to what she was suffering rather than taking away from it, but he also knew that he could not stand by and watch her suffer the way she was doing right now.

It angered him on her behalf that no one else had seen that suffering. Were they all blind, those who purported to care about her, or was it that his love for her made him extra specially perceptive of her feelings? Or was it that she had let down her guard more with him than she ever had with anyone else?

He took a deep breath, knowing that however gently he led up to it nothing was going to make it any easier for either of them.

'Rosie,' he said quietly. 'There's something we need to discuss.'

Rosie heard him, but made no response. Jake paused and, when she made no movement other than to stiffen her already eloquently taut, rejecting back, he cursed under his breath and continued as gently as he could, aching to reach out and touch her, to hold her, to protect her, but knowing that he must not do so.

'The other night you told me that you had conceived Ritchie's child... What happened to that baby?'

Rosie felt the shock like the sudden impact of something so cold that it almost burned. She wasn't prepared for this... hadn't guessed... hadn't imagined. She had thought he wanted to discuss their supposed relationship, not...

Who did he think he was? What was he trying to do to her? Hadn't he hurt her enough... more than enough over the years? What right did he have to pry into this, the most painful and private part of her life... her heart?

She felt the pain burn up inside her, the anger... the guilt... the bitterness.

She turned round, her eyes glittering with a mixture of tears and emotion, her voice raw as she choked out, 'What do you think happened? I killed it... I killed it...'

As he heard the agony in her voice Jake felt his scalp tauten and muscles tense. He could see what she was going through, hear it, feel it, taste it almost, on the emotion-laden air that enveloped her.

Instinctively he wanted to comfort her, to help her, to take away from her the appalling burden of her pain and guilt. She had been a child, that was all, a child whose only guilt had been her own innocence, and yet she was punishing herself as though she had been an adult.

'Rosie. Rosie...you mustn't blame yourself. It wasn't your fault, you were only a child. I know it must have hurt, having to take the decision to have your pregnancy terminated, but——'

He saw the colour leave her face, her mouth twisting in a bitter, corrosive smile.

'But what? I did the right thing? Of course, you *would* think that, wouldn't you? How like a man...' She started to laugh, her voice sharp-edged with a hysteria that sent anxiety arcing through him. 'Well, it wasn't like that. *I* wasn't the one who made the decision. Life...fate...my baby—the baby I'd told constantly since I knew I was carrying it that I hated—was the one who did that...'

Rosie saw from his face that he didn't understand what she was saying.

'I miscarried,' she told him harshly. 'I lost the baby by accident. It knew, you see. It knew it wasn't loved.'

Silently Jake watched the tears pouring down her face, cursing himself for his crassness, his stupidity, his lack of insight. Why on earth hadn't he guessed...realised...? He *loved* her. He should have sensed...known...

For all these years she had contained the pain that was now spilling out from her, years when he could have reached out to her, could have—

should have been there to help her... to hold her... even if it could only have been as a friend.

Why *hadn't* he realised, that day he had gone to see her, to check if there had been any *repercussions* as he had so clinically put it, that she was lying to him, that she was afraid... that she was alone and facing a trauma which would blight her whole life?

If he had not been so wrapped up in his own feelings, his own jealousy, his blind, prejudiced belief that she thought herself to be in love with Ritchie, might he not with his supposed maturity have seen that she was concealing something, that she was afraid?

Couldn't he have found a way to encourage her to confide in him, to lean on him... to draw support from him?

She could have had her baby. He would have gladly provided her with all the support she might have needed... all the love. Given the chance, he would have married her and loved them both, but he had turned his back on her, left her to suffer...

'My baby died because I didn't want it. I killed it by denying it my love... but I did love it...'

He couldn't stand any more.

He crossed the space that divided them, taking her in his arms, ignoring her attempts to push him away, wrapping his arms around her so tightly that she couldn't move, holding her, rocking her, telling her that she wasn't to blame, that these things happened ... that of course she had loved her baby and that of course he or she had known that.

'If anyone is to blame it must be me,' he told her.

Rosie stiffened. 'You ...'

She had stopped crying now, but she was still trembling. Her body felt weak and cold, hollow and empty, drained. She felt much as she had done after her miscarriage, she recognised light-headedly, as though there was an empty space inside her which had previously been filled but, whereas with her miscarriage she had ached with pain over that emptiness, with this one there was a sense of release, of relief.

She tried to concentrate on what Jake was saying. How could it be *his* fault?

'That day when I came to see you ... I should have guessed ... should have seen——'

'But there wasn't anything to see,' Rosie told him. 'I——'

Jake shook his head.

'I didn't mean that kind of "seeing", Rosie ... I meant ...' He stopped abruptly, causing her to frown up at him.

'What?'

'It doesn't matter,' he told her. 'What *does* matter is you, and the way you've blamed yourself ... suffered ... You were very young,

Rosie. Perhaps your body simply wasn't fully ready for motherhood.'

Rosie ducked her head. He was only reiterating what they had told her at the hospital. Then she had felt too much guilt, too much anguish to listen to them, but now logically she knew that both they and he were probably right.

That didn't lessen her sorrow, though. Her sorrow... Not her guilt...not that agonising, clawing mixture of anger and misery which she had been suffering so frequently and intensely recently; that, she recognised, had gone, leaving behind it a kinder, gentler emotion.

Had that change been brought about simply by the act of talking about what had happened, by giving vent to her emotions, by being able for the first time to actually acknowledge what had happened...what she had felt...by acknowledging the right of her child to have a proper place in her past and her memories, instead of being hidden away, his or her existence denied?

Jake was still holding her. She tried to move away discreetly but, far from relaxing, his arms actually seemed to tighten a little more securely around her.

It felt good being held like this by him, her body supported by his, surrounded by its warmth, its protection, his heartbeat soothing the frantic pace of her own. In her dreams she had imagined being held like this, she recognised, had craved this kind of male comfort and warmth, had longed for someone who would hold her, listen to her, understand her...love her...

Immediately she tensed. Jake did *not* love her. He felt compassion for her, and a certain amount of guilt, but he did not love her.

And she was not a child, not a teenager any longer, even if the emotions she had been re-living...venting in his arms had belonged to that era of her life. She was a woman, an adult, and it was time that she put the past behind her, accepted that there was no going back and altering it, accepted that her perceptions of it were coloured by the emotions she had felt then, by the immaturity which had been a part of her then.

She had believed that Jake despised her, condemned her for what she had done, but she had learned now that he had done no such thing. Couldn't she just as easily have allowed her guilt over her miscarriage to be equally biased and destructive? She would never forget her child, never cease regretting that she had lost it, but somehow now that loss was easier to accept, that pain easier to endure now that she shared it with someone else.

For years she had focused all her antipathy and bitterness on Jake; she must not make the mistake now of forcing him to become some kind of emotional support system for her, especially not when she knew that she loved him.

Right now he felt responsible for her...and responsive to her? It would be dangerously easy to use those feelings and to try to convince them both that they could become something else.

Some deep-seated feminine instinct told her that it would be the easiest thing in the world right now to increase Jake's awareness of her, to trade on his obvious compassion for her. All it would take was for her to lift her head, to look at him...to look at his mouth...

She felt the tremor of her own body and acknowledged, with a small pang of shock for her previous lack of awareness, how very strong her physical and emotional responses would be once they were aroused, how very, very much she wanted right now to make love with Jake.

To set the final seal upon the past and free herself completely from it? Or because she loved him...because a part of her was ready to use the smallest excuse it could find to encourage him to want her?

It wouldn't be all that difficult; physically he was responsive to her, aware of her...physically he desired her.

She wasn't sure how she knew that, but she did know it, sensed it, felt it, and in a female way was proud because of it.

But to encourage that desire, to take it and make use of it, would ultimately damage them both, but most especially her. She wasn't strong enough for a relationship which would be based on such a dangerously destructive mixture of compassion and desire on his part, and love and need on hers.

No, if there were ever to be that kind of intimate relationship in her life, then it must be based on emotions that were equally balanced. And besides, to allow... to encourage Jake to make love to her when she knew how widely different their reasons for making love would be would be to cheat and deceive him.

Jake heard her sigh, and felt her lift herself away from him. This time when she pressed firmly against his chest, silently demanding that he release her, he complied.

'I'm sorry,' she told him shakily.

'Don't be,' he responded. 'There's no need.'

He had released her fully now. She was just about to step back from him and turn away when he said softly, 'Rosie...'

'Yes?'

She looked up at him and then tensed as she saw the way he was looking back at her, at her mouth... just as she had so recently imagined he might do.

Quickly she turned on her heel, terrified of giving in to her need to fling herself back into his arms and whisper to him how much she wanted him... loved him.

'I... I must go...'

Jake saw her to her car, and then stood watching her until she had driven out of sight.

The phone was ringing as Rosie let herself into her house. She dropped her bag and ran to answer it, a small thrill of disappointment stabbing through her when she realised it wasn't Jake but Chrissie.

'Rosie... I've had a wonderful idea,' Chrissie announced. 'Why don't you have your engagement party here in the garden? There's masses of room. We could hire a marquee.'

An engagement party. Rosie's heart sank, but she couldn't summon the energy to dampen Chrissie's enthusiasm, nor to destroy the olive branch she knew her sister was extending to her.

'It sounds a marvellous idea,' she fibbed weakly. 'But I'm not sure what Jake's plans are...'

Promising Chrissie that she would discuss the party with him, she replaced the receiver.

Chrissie was *her* sister, she reminded herself, and it was unfair of her to shift the responsibility for persuading her to drop her plans for an engagement party on to Jake's shoulders, but he seemed to have the knack of dealing with her sister. Chrissie listened to him and obviously respected his judgement, while she had always considered Rosie to be her 'little sister' and still tended to treat her accordingly.

An engagement party... Wistfully Rosie tried not to dwell on how different things would be if she and Jake really were planning to marry...if he really did love her.

Enough of that, she told herself firmly. She had plenty of other things to think about, such as work. It was too late to return to the office now, but she had plenty of paperwork she could do here at home.

She went into her sitting-room and switched on the fire, opening the flap of her pretty walnut bureau which she had inherited from her grandmother and sitting down to work.

At nine o'clock Rosie stopped working to make herself a light supper. After she had finished eating and cleared away, she went back to her work, switching on the sitting-room lamps as she did so. The summer light had started to fade, and as she passed in front of her sitting-room window she saw a car coming down the road.

When she realised it was Jake's, her heart missed a beat.

He had probably only come round because Chrissie had been on to him about her wretched party, she told herself as she went to let him in.

She opened the door before he rang the bell, standing back to let him in.

'Has Chrissie——?'

'Rosie, there's something——'

Both of them stopped.

'You first,' Jake offered.

The way he was smiling at her made her feel as though she had suddenly been wrapped in something warm and cherishing, Rosie reflected shakily. It was an unfamiliar experience for her, and a dangerously beguiling one, betraying her into responding to Jake's warmth with a smile that made him catch his breath in love and hope.

Quickly she told him about Chrissie's phone-call, pulling a wry face as she admitted, 'I'm afraid I used you as an excuse for not going ahead.'

'I've had Naomi plaguing me, wanting to know if we've set a wedding date yet,' Jake told her. 'I've referred *her* to you...'

Rosie laughed.

'That wasn't why I came to see you, though...'

Rosie paused in the act of ushering him into her sitting-room.

'I was worried about you...being on your own after what happened this afternoon...' He had turned his head away from her as though half ashamed of his own concern for her, his voice slightly muffled.

As she watched him, Rosie was overwhelmed with emotion. He was so caring, this man, so completely the opposite of all the things she had once thought him. *Why* hadn't she realised sooner...known sooner that...?

That what? That she loved him.

Tears pricked her eyes. This was so unfair... so... so unendurable, after all she had already endured.

She turned her head away from him, afraid that he might somehow read the truth in her eyes.

'That... that was thoughtful of you...'

How formal she sounded, how distant, but she couldn't, dared not, let him see what she was really feeling.

'Rosie... About... about the baby...'

She tensed immediately.

'You have every right to mourn him or her, you know, every right to grieve... Forgive me if I'm saying or doing the wrong thing, but I just wanted you to know that if you can't bring yourself to talk about it to anyone else, someone closer to you... well, I'm always here, you know...'

She hadn't meant it to happen... hadn't planned for it, hadn't encouraged it in any way at all, but as she turned towards him he must have taken a couple of steps towards her.

'Rosie...'

The way he said her name made her whole body quiver. She looked up at him and knew immediately that it was the wrong thing to do.

He wanted her—she could see it in his face, read it in the way his glance dropped slowly to her mouth.

She could have stopped it even then, could have turned away from him, stepped back from him, filled the tense silence with some comment which would have banished the tension between them, but she did none of those things; instead she looked back at him, deliberately letting her own glance linger on his mouth, knowing, as surely as she knew that he could see the warm flush staining her skin, that he knew what she was offering him.

There was no rush, no awkwardness, simply the sensation of being enfolded in his arms, followed by the warmth of his mouth slowly caressing her own, exploring and caressing it, as delicately as though he thought she was something precious and fragile with which he had to take great care.

Hesitantly she opened her mouth and kissed him back, unsure at first, her heart thudding frantically fast; and then, after he had responded to her, shown her, whispered to her how much he wanted her, how much he needed her, her confidence grew, her aching need for him driving out the warning voices urging her to stop now before it was too late.

Only it was already too late. It had been too late from the first moment he touched her. Now she had no defences against the combined emotional and physical longing for him. When he touched her, her body trembled violently in response.

He kissed her mouth and then her throat, his hands warm against her body, tender and patient, not rushing or forcing her. As she clung to him, she could feel the heat coming off his body, sense the desire he was straining to control, but strangely the knowledge of his desire neither alarmed her nor filled her with distaste, as had always been the case in the past with other men.

Neither, when he kissed her, did she see behind her shuttered eyelids an image of his cousin tainting her pleasure in his touch, destroying her ability to respond to him.

'Open your eyes, Rosie,' he told her huskily, as he kissed the corner of each eye. 'I want you to look at me when I touch you. I want you to see *me* when I kiss you... I want you to know who it is who's making love to you.'

Obediently she did as he said, unaware of the effect that her languorously enlarged pupils were having on him.

He touched her face with his hands, cupping it, not daring to let himself touch her body. If he did!

He could feel his own physical response to the thought of touching her, of smoothing his hands over the silky warmth of her skin, of caressing every single inch of her with his mouth, of showing her... giving her all the pleasure she had never known, of helping her to be proud of the sensuality that nature had given her.

He could feel his heart hammering against his ribs, his throat aching with tension and need... He buried his mouth against her throat, feeling her tremble violently against him, seeing in the golden shadow of the lamplight the sudden thrust of her nipples against her clothes.

Heat swamped him. Before he had registered what he was doing, never mind stopped himself, his hands slid to her waist, holding her, his head dipping down, his mouth covering her nipple, caressing it, his mind haunted by his memories of how often he had dreamed of touching her like this.

After one violent shudder of shock, Rosie simply clung quiescently to him, too stunned, too devoured by the physical and emotional sensations his passionate caress had aroused to do anything else.

How could it happen that simply the heat of his mouth, its dampness against her skin, the rough brush of his tongue even through the layers of fabric that separated her flesh from it could cause such a frenzy of sensation inside her, could unleash such an aching, a need, a pulsing, that it was all she could do to stop herself from pressing his head against her breast, from wrenching aside the intrusive fabric that prevented her from experiencing his heated, passionate suckle against her naked flesh?

She wanted to feel him touching her like that, kissing her like that, all over her body, but she had no idea she had voiced that need until he lifted his mouth from her breast and whispered to her, 'Do you, Rosie? Do you? Come here, then, and let me show you how much *I* want to love you like that...'

He had just started to unfasten her blouse when she suddenly shook her head. Immediately his fingers stilled, his eyes watching her, waiting.

'Not here...' she told him huskily, her skin flushing as she looked beyond him towards the half-open door.

It was so hard for her to say the words, to explain to him how she felt...what she wanted, to tell him that, although she knew already that what she would experience with him would be nothing like that other time, she still wanted it to be upstairs in her own bed where, no matter what might happen afterwards, or what the future might hold, she would have the memory of being physically wanted and desired, of being shown tenderness and joy, of knowing what this physical thing between a man and a woman really should be, to destroy for ever the tainted memories of the past.

As she struggled to find the words to express what she was feeling and what she wanted, it

seemed that somehow Jake had read her mind
for her, because he watched her sombrely for a
few seconds and then said quietly, 'No. Not here.'

As she walked nervously towards the door, the
light fell on the damp patch of fabric pulling
tautly against her breast. Heat flooded through
her, weakening her, making her sway slightly on
her feet.

Instantly Jake was holding her, supporting her,
his arm wrapped round her.

They went upstairs in silence.

Outside her bedroom door she paused, hesi-
tating, suddenly filled with doubt and panic.
What if he didn't really want her after all? What
if he was simply doing this because he felt sorry
for her... what if?

As she looked towards him, she saw that he
was very obviously physically aroused; her skin
flushed, her body responding to what she had
seen, filling her with a longing that made her
tremble openly.

She didn't realise Jake had misinterpreted the
reason for that tremor until she heard him saying
softly, 'It's all right, Rosie. You don't have to do
this. If you'd prefer me to leave...'

Her eyes gave her away before she could speak,
filling with such anguish that Jake felt as though
someone was physically tearing at his guts.

He was close to forty years old. He had
promised himself he wouldn't rush her, wouldn't

panic her, wouldn't let his own needs, his own love, get in the way of his desire to help her, to put her first...but when he saw the look of helpless aching, longing dilating her eyes...

'I want to see you,' she told him shakily. 'I want you to see me...'

She stopped speaking, unable to explain that she wanted their intimacy to be open and free, clean and wholesome...shared. That she didn't want it to be something covert and hidden, dark and furtive.

'I want to see you,' she had said, and Jake had heard beneath the defiance in her voice the tiny thread of all her past fear.

He ached in helpless anger and pain for her, but knew that if he voiced what he was feeling she would immediately reject his emotions, driven by pride and the need to protect herself.

Instead he told her wryly, 'There isn't an awful lot to see. A man's body doesn't possess the same beauty as a woman's...' As he spoke he looked down at her, and Rosie felt her heart thud frantically against her ribs as she recognised his desire for her.

Was he saying that he found *her* body beautiful—the swollen curves of her breasts, the swell of her hips, the roundness of her body with its female mysteries?

And he was wrong when he said a man's body did not possess beauty.

His did for her, she recognised as her glance skimmed hesitantly over him. His skin was tanned from the time he had spent in Greece, his arms and legs tautly muscled where hers were more gently structured, his nipples smaller, flatter but, like hers, taut and hard. If she touched them, kissed them, suckled on them, would he experience the same thrill of sensation that his mouth had given her?

Her skin burned at the thought, her hand clenching against her side as she resisted the urge to reach out and touch him, to stroke her fingertips through the soft silk of his body hair, to breathe in the scent of him, to release all her inhibitions and to show him with her hands and her mouth just how much she wanted and needed him.

'Rosie...'

She looked at him, her expression open and unguarded. What he saw in her eyes made Jake reach out for her, groaning helplessly under his breath as his senses reacted to that unspoken message of longing and need.

'Hold me, Rosie,' he whispered against her mouth. 'Hold me ... touch me ... love me ...'

Perhaps after all this was what she needed most: not to be shown the power of her own sexuality, but to be allowed to discover the weakness of his, its vulnerabilities and needs, to be allowed to discover that a man's body was just as vulnerable as a woman's, that she had just as much power to wound and hurt him as he did her, to discover what her touch could do to him.

Against her mouth he whispered thickly, 'Whatever it is you want, Rosie...whatever it is you need, you can have...'

I want *you*, Rosie wanted to tell him. I need you...I love you...but she didn't say the words. Instead she reached out tentatively and touched him, tracing the shape of his shoulder, exploring the warmth of his skin, feeling the way his flesh responded to her touch, seeing in his face that he had told her the truth when he said he wanted her.

What she was learning now...experiencing now were things she should have known years ago, Rosie acknowledged as her heart filled with wonder at the way he reacted to her, at the way he let her see just what she was doing to him, but more unexpected than all of that was the way her own body responded to what she was doing, the way touching him, watching him, kissing him, just simply watching him, aroused her.

When she pressed her lips to the flat plane of his stomach and hesitantly caressed it with the tip of her tongue, the shudder that went through him made her own body ache so sharply that she immediately froze.

'Rosie...it's all right,' Jake started to reassure her, but she shook her head, her face burning with the force of what she was feeling as she took his hand and placed it against her body, and then watched him, uncertainly wondering if she had done the right thing. If she should have waited for him to touch her.

As soon as he touched the moist, intimate heat of her body, Jake knew what was happening to her.

'Rosie...' He kissed her mouth, her breasts, and then her stomach, all the time gently caressing her, trying to fight down his own need so that he could let her body tell him what it wanted...take its own pace.

When he kissed the inside of her thigh she trembled and tensed, but she didn't try to push him away.

His need to touch her, taste her, love her...and to show her what that love could be ached through him.

Rosie... He said her name, helplessly aware of his self-control slipping, unable to resist his need to know her in this most intimate of all physical pleasures, feeling her tense as he opened his mouth over her, telling himself that he would stop the moment she wanted to do, and then becoming so lost in the pleasure of knowing her, tasting her, feeling her body's first quivering response to his intimate caress, that no power on earth could have made him release her.

He felt her body move against him, lifting, twisting...heard her sharp, frantic cries, felt the tug of her fingers in his hair as she tried to push him away, but wouldn't, *couldn't* let her go, not until he had felt the small, sharp quivers of sensation twisting through her body become a series of intense, pulsing contractions that he could physically feel as he caressed her.

Even after it was over, he still caressed her, gently kissing the inside of her thigh, stroking her skin, moving slowly up over her body, touching her, loving her, until he reached her mouth and saw the imprint of her own teeth on her bottom lip and the tears still seeping slowly from her closed eyes.

She was trembling, he recognised, shivering almost like someone in shock. He wrapped his arms round her, holding her, rocking her.

'It's all right, Rosie...it's all right...'

Rosie didn't speak. She couldn't. She was still in shock, still appalled by the intensity of her sexual response to him. Now that she knew...now that he had shown her... How on earth was she ever going to be able to forget?

Panic burned inside her. It would have been bad enough just to know that she loved him emotionally, but now there was this as well. This unwanted knowledge of all the nights ahead of her when she would lie awake, remembering...wanting...aching...knowing that the intensity of the physical peak she had just reached was something that could never be found through mere physical intimacy, that it was something that could only be experienced through love.

Never again would she know the pleasure Jake had just shown her.

She bit down hard on her bottom lip and then cried out as her teeth touched her already bruised skin.

Immediately Jake's hold on her tightened.

'It's all right, Rosie... Go to sleep now... It's all right...'

Go to sleep. How on earth could she sleep? She didn't want to sleep...she wanted... She yawned hugely and then yawned again. Wryly Jake watched her, pillowing her head against his shoulder as her eyes closed, and then reaching out to switch off the light before retrieving the duvet and pulling it over them both.

Rosie woke up abruptly, conscious of something missing, but not sure what it was until her brain cleared and she realised she was on her own.

'Jake...' She said his name sharply, not really expecting any response, tensing when he suddenly appeared in the open doorway.

She stared at him in the semi-darkness, her heart beating fast.

'I...I thought you'd gone.'

Thought or hoped? Jake wondered grimly as he walked towards her and sat down on the edge of the bed.

He had broken all the rules, done all the things he had promised himself he would not do, and now he was going to lose her—he could see it in her eyes. She could hardly bear to even look at him.

'Rosie——' he began, but she wouldn't let him speak, interrupting him, saying fiercely,

'You don't have to say anything, Jake. It should never have happened. We both know that. It was all my fault . . . I should never——'

'*Your* fault . . .? If any blame lies with anyone, it lies with me, not you, Rosie.'

She turned to look at him. He could see the way her eyes shone in the dark, feel her tension and vulnerability. She didn't seem to realise that as she sat up the duvet had slid away from her body, or was it that she simply didn't realise what effect the sight of her naked breasts was having on him?

'*I* was the one who started it,' he reminded her gently.

'But I didn't stop you . . . I wanted . . .' Rosie bit her lip, shaking her head, knowing how close she had just come to blurting out how she felt about him.

'I'm not a total fool,' she told him stiffly. 'I do know that sex is different for men than it is for women... that a man doesn't necessarily have to feel any emotional involvement with a woman... to... to want to have sex with her...'

It was like trying to pick his way across a mine-field, Jake recognised as he tried to unravel what she was really saying to him.

'Not to have sex,' he agreed, watching her, wondering if that really had been pain he had seen in her eyes before she turned her head away from him or whether he was deluding himself.

What more did he have to lose? he asked himself grimly. Only his pride, and what the hell did that matter?

'Not to have sex, Rosie,' he repeated, reaching out and gently cupping her face, sliding his hand along her jaw and firmly turning her face towards his own. 'But to make love... that's dif-ferent... and I did make love with you, Rosie, even if *you* only had sex with me.'

She had gone very still and silent, her face showing no trace of emotion or reaction at all.

'And I do love you, Rosie... have loved you for a very long time...' his mouth twisted wryly '...a very long time. Have you any idea what it does to a man to have to admit that he's fallen in love with someone who's still virtually a child, even if physically she might look like a woman? Have you any idea what it did to me to find you in bed with Ritchie?'

Now she did show some reaction, her body tensing, pain flickering in her eyes.

'You don't have to say this to me, you know,' she told him fiercely. 'I'm not going to fall apart just because I've suddenly discovered that I love you, Jake. You don't have to feel sorry for me . . . to pretend . . .'

For a moment he was too stunned to speak, to take in her muffled, fiercely spoken words.

'I know why you made love to me, you know,' she continued without looking at him, her words low and rushed. 'I know you did it because of . . . of Ritchie. I know you just wanted . . . don't want your pity, Jake,' she told him harshly. 'I don't want——'

'What?' he demanded savagely, his control suddenly deserting him as he grabbed hold of her shoulders and almost shook her. 'You don't want what, Rosie? Me . . . my body, my need, my desire, my love . . . ? Well, you've got them whether you want them or not, and I'll tell you something else, shall I? All those things you don't want from me, I *do* want from you . . . all of them and more. I want you, Rosie. I want your emotions, your needs, your desires . . . your love . . . your life . . . I want all of it. All of it . . . all of you, and if you say one word more to me about pity or compassion——' He stopped abruptly, shaking his head. 'Rosie, I'm sorry . . . I shouldn't——'

He felt her hand tremble as she reached out and touched his mouth.

'No... No more words,' she told him thickly. 'Don't tell me, Jake... Show me... show me...'

He could feel the way her body shook as she kissed him and wound herself around him, the small frantic kisses that betrayed her emotions and aroused his own.

This time, when he made love to her, it was the powerful pulse of his body within her own that brought her to the peak of her own pleasure.

Later, snuggled up against him, she heard him murmur in her ear, 'That marquee Chrissie was talking about... How about using it to celebrate our wedding?'

'So soon?' Rosie protested. 'My parents——'

'They'll be there. Chrissie will see to that, and besides...' In the darkness he kissed her gently and then touched her stomach. Immediately Rosie knew what he meant.

'I wouldn't want our child to think it wasn't conceived in love any more than I would want you to think it,' he told her softly.

Chrissie was overjoyed when they told her the news.

'Leave everything to me,' she told them firmly.

'What's this?' Rosie asked Jake uncertainly as he handed her a small, gift-wrapped box.

They had been married just over three months, and she had never been happier. The shadows thrown by the past had completely disappeared and no longer held any fear or threat for her. They had just come back from a fortnight's holiday in Greece, Jake having decided to retain his interest in the marina project but to take a smaller active part in its management.

'I don't want to be away from you,' he had told Rosie when they had discussed it. 'Your own business means that you won't always be free to come with me...'

And so, rather than ask her to put their relationship before her work, he had been the one to make that decision and that choice.

'You're more important to me than anything else in my life, Rosie,' he had told her. 'I've loved you for too long, wanted you for too long, to let anything come between us now that we are together.'

She hadn't told him yet that she suspected she was soon going to have to look for a partner to take over her role in her business because she had conceived their child.

Now, as she unwrapped the gift he had given her and saw the small gold teddy bear dangling from its delicate chain, she wondered if somehow he had guessed after all, but then he said quietly, 'I'm not sure if I've got the dates right... I thought it must have been about this time...' and she realised that this gift wasn't for the child *they* had conceived together, but for the one she had secretly lost.

Tears burned her eyes as she went into his arms.

'I don't ever want you to think you can't grieve for him...talk about him,' he told her huskily as he held her. 'Or that I've forgotten what you went through...what you suffered...or how I wasn't there for you when you most needed me.'

Rosie shook her head. 'Oh, Jake...'

'Don't think I don't realise what it must have cost you to have Ritchie here when we got married. To treat him normally...to——'

'Ritchie doesn't bother me,' Rosie told him truthfully. 'If you want the truth...what happened with him...it doesn't worry me any more, Jake. Losing my baby—that was different, although I accept now that it wasn't necessarily because I'd willed it to happen. You've driven out all my bad memories and replaced them with good ones.'

She kissed him and then smiled mischievously at him. 'It's a pity you bought this, though...' she told him.

'A pity?' Instantly he frowned. 'Rosie——'

'Because now you're going to have to buy another one,' she told him, watching his face as he realised what she was actually saying.

'Are you pleased?' she asked him after he had finished kissing her.

'Pleased?' He held her tightly, his voice raw with emotion as he told her, 'You're having my child. Pleased doesn't come anywhere near describing how I feel.

'I loved you for so long without thinking you could ever love me, Rosie. Sometimes I still can't quite believe that any of this is real, and then I look at you, hold you... touch you... love you, and I see in your eyes that it is real, that you do love me.

'Of course I'm pleased,' he whispered against her mouth. 'Come here and let me show you how much...'

'Mm... That sounds like a good idea to me... A very good idea,' she whispered dreamily against his mouth as he began to kiss her.

Take 4 bestselling love stories FREE
Plus get a FREE surprise gift!

Special Limited-time Offer

Mail to Harlequin Reader Service®

3010 Walden Avenue
P.O. Box 1867
Buffalo, N.Y. 14269-1867

YES! Please send me 4 free Harlequin Presents® novels and my free surprise gift. Then send me 6 brand-new novels every month, which I will receive months before they appear in bookstores. Bill me at the low price of $2.66 each plus 25¢ delivery and applicable sales tax, if any*. That's the complete price and a savings of over 10% off the cover prices—quite a bargain! I understand that accepting the books and gift places me under no obligation ever to buy any books. I can always return a shipment and cancel at any time. Even if I never buy another book from Harlequin, the 4 free books and the surprise gift are mine to keep forever.

108 BPA AW6U

Name	(PLEASE PRINT)	
Address		Apt. No.
City	State	Zip

This offer is limited to one order per household and not valid to present Harlequin Presents® subscribers. *Terms and prices are subject to change without notice. Sales tax applicable in N.Y.

UPRES-995 ©1990 Harlequin Enterprises Limited

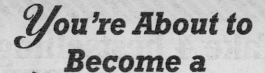

You're About to Become a

Privileged Woman

Reap the rewards of fabulous free gifts and benefits with proofs-of-purchase from Harlequin and Silhouette books

Pages & Privileges™

It's our way of thanking you for buying our books at your favorite retail stores.

PROOF OF PURCHASE
HP-PP79
Offer expires October 31, 1996

Harlequin and Silhouette— the most privileged readers in the world!

For more information about Harlequin and Silhouette's PAGES & PRIVILEGES program call the Pages & Privileges Benefits Desk: 1-503-794-2499

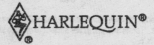

HARLEQUIN®

HP-PP79